Maybe Not

Also by Colleen Hoover

Maybe Not

A Novella

Colleen Hoover

ATRIA PAPERBACK

NEW YORK LONDON TORONTO SYDNEY NEW DELHI

ATRIA PAPERBACK

An Imprint of Simon & Schuster, Inc.
1230 Avenue of the Americas
New York, NY 10020

First Atria Paperback edition December 2015

ATRIA PAPERBACK and colophon are trademarks of
Simon & Schuster, Inc.

The Simon & Schuster Speakers Bureau can bring authors to your
live event. For more information or to book an event, contact the
Simon & Schuster Speakers Bureau at 1-866-248-3049
or visit our website at www.simonspeakers.com.

ISBN 978-1-5011-2571-3
ISBN 978-1-4767-9984-1 (ebook)

To Kendall Smith, one of my very best friends. You've been by my side since we were kids, and I couldn't do any of this without you.

Maybe Not

Chapter One

I'm convinced that hell has an intercom system and the buzz of my alarm clock is played at full volume on repeat against the screams of all the lost souls.

Which is why I'll never murder anyone, because there's no way I can live with this sound for eternity. I can't even live with it for five seconds.

I reach over and stop the alarm, dreading another day at work. I hate that I have to keep this shitty barista job just to pay for school. At least Ridge lets my sporadic rent checks slide in exchange for my managing his band. It works for now, but *God, I hate mornings.*

I stretch my arms, bring my hands to my eyes, and begin rubbing the sleep out of them. When my fingers meet my eyes, for a split second I think maybe my worst fears have come true and I'm actually burning in hell, because *SHIT! Motherfucker! I'm going to kill him!*

"Ridge!" I scream.

Oh, God. It burns.

I stand up and attempt to open my eyes, but they're stinging too badly for them to be of any use. It's the oldest prank in the book, and I can't believe I fell for it. *Again.*

I can't find my shorts—*God, it hurts so bad*—so I stumble my way to the bathroom in order to wash the pepper juice from my eyes and hands. I find the doorknob and swing the door open, rushing straight to the sink. I'm pretty sure I hear a girl screaming, but that very well could be *me* screaming.

I cup my hands beneath the stream of water and bring them up to my eyes, rinsing them over and over until the burn starts to subside. Once my eyes begin to feel relief, my shoulder starts to ache from the repeated blows being delivered to it.

"Get out, you pervert!"

I'm awake enough now to know that I actually did hear a girl screaming, and now that girl is hitting me. In *my* bathroom.

I grab a hand towel and press it to my eyes while I shield her punches with my elbow.

"I was peeing, you sick bastard! Get out!"

Shit, she hits hard. I still can't really see her, but I can recognize fists when they're flying at me. I grab both of her wrists to keep her from assaulting me even more.

"Stop hitting me!" I yell.

The bathroom door that leads to the living room swings open and my left eye is working enough that I can tell Brennan is standing there. "What the hell is going on?" He walks toward us and removes my hands from her wrists and then stands between us. I bring the towel back to my eyes and squeeze them shut.

"He barged in on me while I was peeing!" the girl yells. "And he's naked!"

I open one eye and glance down. I am, in fact, completely naked.

"Jesus, Warren. Put on some clothes," Brennan says.

"How was I supposed to know I'd be attacked in my own bathroom?" I say, pointing at her. "Why the hell is she using my bathroom, anyway? Your guests can use *your* bathroom."

Brennan immediately holds up two defensive palms. "She didn't spend the night with me."

"Gross," the girl mutters.

I don't know why Ridge thought it would be a good idea to rent a four-bedroom apartment. Even though one of the bedrooms is empty, that's still two people too many. Especially when guests spend the night and don't know about the designated bathrooms.

"Look," I say, pushing both of them toward the door that leads to the living room. "This is my bathroom and I'd like to use it. I don't care where she slept or who she slept with; she can use your bathroom. This one's mine."

Brennan holds up a finger and turns to face me. "Actually," he says, "this is a *shared* bathroom. With *that* bedroom." He points to the door that leads to the other bedroom. "And that bedroom now belongs to . . ." He points to the girl. "Bridgette. Your new roommate."

I pause.

Why did he just call her my roommate?

"What do you mean, *roommate*? No one asked me if I wanted a new roommate."

Brennan shrugs. "You rarely pay rent, Warren. You don't really have a say in who lives here."

He knows I don't pay rent because I help manage their band, but Ridge does take on the brunt of the financial expenses. He makes a good point, unfortunately.

This isn't good. I can't share a bathroom with a girl.

Especially a girl with that good of an arm. And especially a girl with all that bronzed skin.

I look away from her. I hate that she's hot. I hate that she's a brunette, because I really like her long, light brown hair and the way it's pulled back, all messy and shit.

Dammit!

"Well, this has been a really fun bonding moment," Bridgette says, walking toward me. She shoves my shoulders, pushing me back toward my bedroom. "Now wait your turn, *Roomie*."

The bathroom door closes in my face and I'm standing in my room again. Still naked. And maybe a little emasculated.

"You can leave, too," I hear her say to Brennan, right before the door to the living room slams shut. Seconds later, the water begins running in the shower.

She's in the shower.

My shower.

She's probably taking off her shirt right now, tossing it on the floor, pulling her panties down over her hips.

I'm fucked.

My apartment is my sanctuary. My man cave. The only place I can go where my life isn't ruled by women. My boss is a woman, all my professors are women, my sister and my mother are both women. Once Bridgette steps into my shower and makes it her own with all her girly shampoos and razors and shit, I'm screwed. That's *my* shower.

I walk to Ridge's bedroom and flip the light switch a couple of times to give him warning that I'm coming in, since he's deaf and can't hear me knocking or stomping toward his room like a kid about to tattle on his little brother.

I flip the switch two more times and then swing his door open. He's lifting up onto his elbows, groggy-eyed. He sees the anger on my face and he begins to laugh, incorrectly assuming I'm here about the pepper-juice prank.

I hate that I fell for it. I'm such a deep sleeper though, and he gets me every damn time.

"That prank was stupid," I sign to him. "But I'm not here because of that. We need to talk."

He sits up in bed and reaches over to tilt his alarm clock so that he can check the time. He looks back at me, agitated. "It's six-thirty in the morning," he signs. "What the hell do you want to talk about at six-thirty in the morning?"

I point in the direction of the new roommate's bedroom. *Bridgette.*

I hate her name.

"You let a *girl* move in?" I make the sign for roommate and continue. "Why in the world would you let a *girl* move in with us?"

Ridge makes the sign for Brennan's name. "That's all him. I don't think he would have accepted no for an answer."

I laugh. "Since when are girls important to Brennan?"

"I heard that," Brennan says from behind me. "*And* saw you sign it."

I face him. "Good. So answer the question."

He glares at me and then looks at Ridge. "Go back to sleep. I'll handle the five-year-old." He motions for me to follow him into the living room, turning out Ridge's bedroom light as he exits.

I like Brennan, but the fact that we've known each other for so long makes me feel like he's my little brother sometimes. My *annoying-as-fuck* little brother. My little brother who thinks moving his women into our apartment is a good idea.

"It's just for a few months," Brennan says, continuing toward the kitchen. "She's in a rough spot and needs a place to stay."

I follow Brennan into the kitchen. "Since when did you start providing rescue homes? You don't even let girls spend the night when you're done with them, much less move in with you. Are you in love with her or something? Because if that's the case, this is the stupidest decision you've ever made. You'll get tired of her in a week, and then what?"

Brennan faces me and calmly holds up a finger. "I told you earlier, it's not like that. We aren't together and we never will be together. But she's important to me and she's in a tough spot and we're going to help her, okay?" He takes a bottle of water out of the fridge and opens the cap. "It won't be that bad. She's in school and works full-time, so she'll hardly ever be here. You won't even notice."

I groan, frustrated, and run my hands down my face. "This is great," I mumble. "The last thing I need right now is some chick taking over my entire bathroom."

Brennan rolls his eyes and begins walking back toward his bedroom. "It's a *bathroom*, Warren. You're acting like a little shit."

"She *hit* me!" I say in defense.

Brennan turns and cocks an eyebrow. "See what I mean?" He walks into his bedroom and closes the door behind him.

The water turns off in the shower, and I hear the curtain slide open. As soon as the door to her bedroom shuts, I walk toward the bathroom. *My* bathroom. I try to open the door from the living room, but it's locked from the inside. I walk through my bedroom and check that door, but it's locked, too. I walk out of my room, straight into her bedroom. My eyes catch a glimpse of her before she screams and pulls a towel in front of her.

"What the hell are you *doing*?"

She picks up a shoe and tosses it at me. It hits me in the shoulder, but I don't even flinch. I ignore her and walk into the bathroom and slam the door shut. I lean against it, lock it behind me, and then close my eyes.

Dammit, she's hot.

Why does she have to be hot?

And I know it was just a glimpse but . . . she shaves. *Everywhere.*

It's bad enough I have to share a bathroom with a girl, but now I have to share it with a *hot* girl? A hot girl who has a severe mean streak? A hot girl with a sick tan and hair so long and thick, it covers up her breasts when it's wet, and *shit, shit, shit.*

I hate Brennan. I hate Ridge. I also love them for doing this to me.

Maybe having her for a roommate could be a good thing.

"Hey, asshole!" she yells through the door. "I used all the hot water. Have fun."

Maybe not.

I walk to Brennan's room and swing open the door. He's packing a suitcase and doesn't even look at me when I stalk over to him.

"What now?" he asks, annoyed.

"I need to ask you something and I need you to be completely honest with me."

He sighs and turns to face me. "What is it?"

"Have you slept with her?"

He looks at me like I'm an idiot. "I already told you no."

I hate that he's acting so mature and calm about this situation, because my reaction is making me feel really immature. Brennan has always been the immature one. Since the moment I met Ridge . . . *God, how long ago was that? Ten years? I'm twenty-four, Brennan's twenty-one . . . yeah. Ten years.* I've been best friends with them for a decade, and this is the first time I've actually felt inferior to Brennan.

I don't like it. *I'm* the responsible one. Well, not as responsible as Ridge, obviously, but no one is. I do manage Brennan's band, and I do a hell of a good job of it, so why can't I seem to control my reactions right now?

Because. I know myself, and if I can't get rid of the new roommate right away, then I'll more than likely become infatuated with her. And if I'll be infatuated with her, I need to make sure Brennan *isn't*.

"You have to be honest with me, because I think you might be in love with her and I need you to tell me you're not, because I think I might want to kiss her. And touch her. A lot. Like, everywhere."

Brennan's hands fly to his forehead and he looks at me like I've lost my mind. He takes several steps back.

"Are you listening to yourself, Warren? I mean, *fuck*, man! You yell at me three minutes ago because you hate her and don't want her here, and now you're saying you want her? Are you bipolar?"

He makes a good point.

Jesus, what's wrong with me?

I pace the room, trying to figure out a solution. She can't stay here. But I want her to stay. I can't share a bathroom with her, but I don't really want anyone else to share a bathroom with her, either. I'm a little bit selfish, apparently.

I pause my frantic pacing and look at Brennan. "Why is she so *mean*?"

Brennan walks over to me and calmly places two hands on my shoulders. "Warren Russell, you need to calm the hell down. You're starting to freak me out."

I shake my head. "I know. I'm sorry, I just. I don't want to be attracted to a girl that you're involved with, so I need to know now if that's the case because we go too far back to let something like this mess us up. But you also know you can't just drop a girl that looks like her in my lap, and expect me not to go there in my head. And I just saw her naked and now I'm useless. Ruined. She's so damn perfect beneath all those clothes and . . ." I look up at him. "I just want to make sure I'm not stepping on any toes when I fantasize about her tonight."

Brennan stares at me, mulling over my admission. He pats me twice on the shoulder and returns to his suitcase. "She's mean, Warren. Probably the meanest girl I've ever met in my life. So if she murders you in your sleep, don't say I didn't warn you." He closes his suitcase and begins to zip it. "She needed a place to stay and we have an extra room. Her life makes mine and Ridge's look like a cakewalk, so go easy on her."

I take a seat on the edge of his bed. I'm trying to be sympathetic to the situation, but the business manager in me is skeptical. "She just called you out of the blue and asked if she could move in with you? Don't you think that's a little suspicious, Brennan? You don't think it has to do with the band finally making a name for itself?"

Brennan glares at me. "She's not an opportunist, Warren. Trust me on that. And hit on her if you want, I couldn't care less."

He walks toward the door and grabs his keys off the dresser. "I'll be back next week after the last show. Do you have our hotel rooms squared up?"

I nod. "I emailed you all the confirmation numbers."

"Thanks," he says as he walks out of the room.

I fall back onto the bed and hate the fact that Brennan isn't into her. That means she's fair game.

I was kind of hoping she wasn't.

But then I smile, because she is.

Chapter Two

"What are you doing?" Ridge signs.

I walk back to Bridgette's bedroom with another glass of water. Once I carefully place it on the floor with all the others, I come back to the living room. "She's lived here two weeks," I tell Ridge. "If she wants to be a roommate, she has to live with the pranks. It's the rule."

Ridge shakes his head disapprovingly.

"What?" I say defensively.

He sighs heavily. "She hardly seems like the type to embrace pranks. This will backfire on you. She hasn't even spoken to us since she moved in."

I disagree with a shake of my head. "She hasn't spoken to *you* because you're deaf and she doesn't know sign language. She hasn't spoken to me because I'm pretty sure I intimidate her."

"You *annoy* her," Ridge signs. "I don't think that girl is capable of being intimidated."

I shake my head. "I don't annoy her. I think she might be attracted to me and that's why she's avoiding me. Because she knows it's not a good idea for roommates to hook up."

Ridge points to her bedroom. "Then why are you making an effort to prank her? Do you *want* her to speak to you? Because if you think roommates shouldn't hook up, then you probably shouldn't be . . ."

I interrupt him. "I didn't say *I* think roommates shouldn't hook up. I said I think that's why she's avoiding me."

"So you want to hook up with her?"

I roll my eyes. "You don't get it. No, I don't want to hook up with her. Yes, I like staring at her ass. And I'm only pranking her because if she's going to live here, she needs to get used to it. When in Rome . . ."

Ridge throws his hands up in defeat and heads toward his room, just as the front door begins to open. I rush to my bedroom and shut the door before she sees me.

I sit on the bed and wait.

And I wait.

And I wait some more.

I lie down on the bed. I wait some more.

She never makes a sound. I don't hear her getting angry that I just filled over fifty cups of water and placed them strategically around her entire bedroom. I don't hear her stomping into the kitchen to pour them out. I don't hear her beating on my door to throw the cups of water at my face in retaliation.

I'm so confused.

I stand up and walk out of my bedroom, but she's not in the kitchen or living room. Her work shoes are by the front door where she keeps them, so I know she came home. I know she went into her room.

What a disappointment. Her lack of response makes me feel like my prank was a failure, when I know it wasn't. It was epic. There's no way she could have made it one foot into her room without having to move all those cups of water.

I stalk back to my bedroom and lie down on the bed.

I want to be pissed at her. I want to hate her for sucking at prank retaliation.

But I don't. I can't stop smiling because I love that her response caught me off guard. She's unexpected, and I like that.

• • •

"Warren."

Her voice sounds so sweet. I must be dreaming.

"Warren, wake up."

So, so sweet. Angelic, even.

I give myself a few seconds to adjust to her voice, to the fact that she's waking me up, to the randomness of her being at my bedroom door, calling out my name. I slowly open my eyes and roll onto my back. I lift up onto my elbows and look at her. She's standing in the doorway between the bedroom and our bathroom. She's wearing an oversized Sounds of Cedar T-shirt, and it doesn't even look like she's wearing anything underneath it.

"What's up?" I ask her.

She wants me. She totally wants me.

She folds her arms tightly over her chest. She tilts her head to the side, and I watch as her eyes narrow into tiny, angry slits. "Don't ever step foot inside my bedroom again. *Ass*hole." She straightens up and backs into the bathroom, slamming the door.

I glance at the clock, and it's two in the morning. That was an extremely delayed reaction to my prank. Was she just waiting for me to fall asleep so she could wake me up and yell at me? Is that her idea of revenge?

She's such an amateur.

I smile to myself and roll over, shifting on the bed. I gasp when a rush of water pours down on top of me.

What the fuck?

I look up, just as an empty cup falls from the edge of the headboard and hits me square between the eyes.

I close my eyes, ashamed that I didn't see that coming. I'm so disappointed in myself. And now I'll have to sleep on towels, because my mattress is soaking wet.

I throw the covers off and swing my legs over the bed, only for my feet to be met with even more cups of water. I knock several of them over in my attempt to stand and it creates a sort of domino effect. I bend over and try to stop them from falling over, but I just make it worse. She's placed them so close together, all over my bedroom floor, and I can't find a safe spot to step.

I try to reach for the nightstand while at the same time lifting my right leg so that it doesn't hit any more cups, but I lose my balance in the process and . . . *yes*. I fall down. Onto the remaining pile of cups that are full of water. Water that is now all over my carpet.

Touché, Bridgette.

•   •   •

I'm carrying the cups of water from my bedroom to the kitchen, back and forth, back and forth. Ridge is sitting at the table, staring at me. I know he wants to ask why the cups are now in my room, but he better not. I'm sure he can see by the look on my face that I don't need his *"I told you so."*

The door to Bridgette's bedroom opens and she walks

out with her backpack slung over her shoulder. I pause and stare at her for a few seconds. Her hair is pulled back into a ponytail. She has on a pair of jeans and a blue tank top. She's usually wearing her Hooters uniform, which, don't get me wrong, is fantastic. But this? Seeing her dressed down with her flip-flops on and no makeup is just . . . *Stop looking at her.*

"Good morning, Warren," she says, shooting daggers in my direction. She glances at the cups in my hands. "Sleep well?"

I smile at her with vengeance. "Screw you, Bridgette."

She crinkles up her nose and gives her head a quick shake. "No thanks," she says, heading toward the front door. "Oh, by the way. We're out of toilet paper. Also, I couldn't find my razor, so I hope you don't mind that I used yours." She opens the front door and turns to face me. "And . . ." She scrunches up her nose again. "I accidentally knocked your toothbrush into the toilet. Sorry. I rinsed it off for you, though."

She closes the door right when one of the cups of water flies out of my hand and meets the back of the door.

She's such a bitch.

Ridge calmly walks past me, straight to his bedroom. He doesn't even look at me, because he knows me better than anyone, and therefore, he knows not to speak to me right now.

I wish Brennan knew me that well, because he's laughing, making his way into the kitchen. Every time he glances up at me, he laughs even harder. "I know she's mean, but Christ, Warren. She *hates* you." He's still laughing as he opens the dishwasher to unload it. "I mean, really hates you."

I finish the trek across the living room and set the empty cups next to the sink. "I can't do this anymore," I say to him. "I can't live with a girl."

Brennan glances at me, amused. He doesn't think I'm serious.

"Tonight. I want her out tonight. She can move in with a friend, or with that sister of hers she's always on the phone with. I want her gone, Brennan."

He can see that I'm not kidding. He straightens up and presses his hands onto the counter behind him, eyeing me. He shakes his head. "She's not leaving."

He reaches down and closes the dishwasher and presses the button to start it. He begins to walk away so I follow after him. "You can't have final say in who lives here. I've tried for two weeks to get along with her, and she's fucking impossible."

Brennan glances at all the cups lining the countertop. "You think pranking her is making an effort to get along with her?" He looks back at me. "You have a hell of a lot to learn about women, Warren." He turns away from me and walks back toward his room. "She's not leaving. She's our roommate now, so *deal* with it."

He slams his door, and it pisses me off even more because I'm really tired of everyone slamming doors lately. I stomp across the living room and swing his door open. "Either she goes or I go!"

As soon as I say it, I regret it. Actually, I don't. I'm not going anywhere, but maybe the threat will change his mind. He shrugs.

"See ya," he says casually.

I turn around and punch the door. "Seriously, Brennan? You would let me leave over her?"

He stands and walks toward me, not stopping until we're eye to eye. "Yes, Warren. I would. So go think it over and let me know when you're moving out." His hand grips the door and he tries to close it in my face, but I slap my palm against it and push it back open.

"You're fucking her," I say.

"Stop it, already! I'm not fucking her."

My jaw is clenched tightly and I'm nodding my head slowly. That's the only explanation for why he's endlessly defending her. "I don't know why you won't just admit it, Brennan. It's fine. You're in love with Bridgette and you don't want her to move out. If you would just admit it, I'd stop."

Brennan's jaw tenses and he expels a quick, frustrated breath. He runs his hands through his hair, and that's when I see it. I see it written all over his face.

Brennan is in love with Bridgette.

I don't know how I feel about that, which makes no sense, since I'm trying to kick her out.

"Warren," he says calmly. He backs into the room and motions for me to step inside. I don't know why he thinks he needs privacy when the only other person in this apartment is Ridge. He closes the door behind me once I'm inside his bedroom. He puts his hands on his hips and stares at the floor for several seconds. When his eyes finally meet mine again, they're full of defeat.

I knew it.

"I'm not in love with Bridgette," he says calmly. "She's my sister."

Chapter Three

I'm pacing the room, holding my forehead, pausing every few feet to look at Brennan and shake my head, only to continue pacing again.

I liked it better when I thought he was fucking her.

"How?" I ask. "How is that even possible?" I pause again and face him. "And why didn't you guys tell me before now?" I feel slightly excluded, like Ridge and Brennan were trying to keep some big family secret from me. That isn't right, because *I'm* their family. They lived with me after they left home. My parents took them in and gave them a roof over their heads and food on the table.

"Ridge doesn't know," Brennan says. "And I don't want him to know until we find out for sure. We'll have a paternity test done soon, but our schedules just haven't worked out yet and it's kind of expensive."

Great. I can't keep secrets from Ridge. We've been best friends since we were ten. I've never kept a secret from him, especially one this big.

"Warren, swear to me you won't tell him. The last thing he needs right now is more stress, and if he finds out I've been in touch with our father, he'll take it personally."

My hands fly up in the air. "Your father, Brennan? Why in the hell would you ever want to contact that bastard again?"

He shakes his head. "I didn't. After Bridgette found out that her biological mother had an affair with our father, she found me and asked me to help her find him." He folds his arms over his chest and looks down at the floor. "I warned her, but she had to see it for herself. I won't be seeing my father again, but if Ridge knows I even took her to see him, he would think I was going behind his back to reach out to our parents, and I wasn't."

"What did your father say when you showed up after all these years?"

Ridge and Brennan moved in with me and my parents when they were only seventeen and fourteen, so it's been about seven years since either of them has had contact with their father.

Brennan shakes his head. "He hasn't changed. He barely said two sentences to us before he sent us on our way. I think it disappointed her so much, she'd be fine not having a paternity test completed if it weren't for Ridge and me possibly being her brothers. I think she just wants someone she can call family, which is why I'm helping her out with all this. I feel bad for her."

I can't believe this. I never would have guessed it. "She doesn't even look like either of you." Brennan and Ridge look almost identical, and they both look just like their father. If their father is the common link between them and Bridgette, you would think she'd have some form of similarity to them. Other than her brown hair, there's nothing about her that looks like Ridge or Brennan. Her green eyes aren't even close to their dark brown eyes, so if she is their sister, she must have taken a hundred percent after her mother. I could just be justifying the fact that I don't want them to look alike. That would be a little strange for me.

Brennan shrugs. "We still don't know for sure, Warren. If it turns out she's not his daughter, then Ridge will never even have to know about this."

I nod, knowing full well that Brennan is right. Ridge has enough on his plate having to deal with Maggie's issues, and until they know for sure, this isn't something he should have to stress over.

"What happens to Bridgette?" I ask him. "If it turns out she's not your sister."

Brennan shrugs. "Then I guess she's just our new roommate."

I sit down on the bed and try to soak everything in. This changes everything. If she's Ridge and Brennan's sister, she won't just be my roommate. She and her attitude and her tiny little Hooters shorts will be part of our lives forever.

I don't really know how I feel about that.

"Are you sure she's not just trying to swindle you?"

Brennan rolls his eyes. "That girl is just trying to survive, Warren. She's had a really fucked-up life, and even if it turns out we're not related, she just needs someone to give her a chance. So please. You don't even have to be nice to her. Just be understanding enough to allow her to live here."

I nod and fall back onto the bed. *Sister?*

"So," I say to Brennan. "I guess that means you definitely aren't into her. Which means I *can* be."

Brennan's pillow meets my face. "You're disgusting."

Chapter Four

Brennan was right. I'm disgusting. I've never felt more disappointed in myself than I have these past two weeks. Since the moment I found out she might be Ridge and Brennan's sister, I haven't been able to stop staring at her. I keep trying to pinpoint mannerisms they have in common, or physical features, but the only thing I've noticed is how hot she looks in that Hooters outfit.

Which, in turn, makes me disgusted with myself, because thoughts of her in her uniform lead to some really strange dreams. Last night I dreamt I walked into the apartment and she was standing in the kitchen in those tiny orange shorts with her midriff showing. But when my eyes made it to her face, it wasn't her face I was looking at. It was Brennan's. He was smiling at me with a shit-eating grin, and right when I started gagging, Ridge walked out of his room wearing the same Hooters outfit.

I woke up after that and had to immediately go to the bathroom and brush my teeth. I don't know why I thought brushing my teeth would help me, but whatever. This sibling thing is fucking with my head in more ways than it should. On the one hand, I think it would be cool if Ridge and Brennan had a sister. On the other hand, I don't want that sister to be Bridgette. Mainly because I'm skeptical of the reasons she's showing up out of the blue right when Brennan begins to make a name for himself. Does she have ulterior motives? Does she think he's made of money?

Because as the band's manager, I can assure her, he's not. The money the band brings in goes right back into promotion and travel expenses. It's at the point where they're putting in so much time and effort, if it doesn't start paying off during this next scheduled tour, it may be the last one they go on. Which is why I'm a little bitter when it comes to Bridgette, because I need Brennan's focus to be on Sounds of Cedar and Ridge's focus to be on writing the songs. I don't want them caught up in family drama.

But dammit. Those shorts.

I'm standing in my bedroom doorway, watching her. She's in the kitchen, talking on the phone while she makes herself something to eat. The phone is sitting on the counter and she's on speaker with whoever is on the other line.

Bridgette hasn't noticed I'm standing here, so until she does, I'm staying right here. Because seeing her have a normal, human conversation is something I've never witnessed before, and I can't stop watching. Which is strange, because how many times a day do I see people having typical interactions with other humans? It says a lot about Bridgette's personality that seeing her do something like this could actually be fascinating. She'd make an interesting anthropological study, considering she doesn't seem to conform to how society expects a young woman to act.

"I can't take living in this dorm," the voice on speaker says. "My roommate's a fruit loop dingus."

Bridgette tilts her head toward the direction of the

phone, but still doesn't turn around to see me. "You can make it until you graduate."

"And then we can get our own place?"

My ears perk up, hearing her mention the possibility of moving out. "We can't afford our own place," Bridgette says.

"We could if you would go back into doing porn films."

"It was one porn," Bridgette says defensively. "We needed the money. Besides, I was in it for all of three minutes, so will you please stop bringing it up."

Holy shit. *Please say the name, please say the name.* I have to know the name of this porn.

"Okay, okay," the girl says, laughing. "I'll stop bringing it up if you can promise I'll be out of the dorms in three months."

Bridgette shakes her head. "You know I don't make promises. And are you forgetting about the time we tried living together for three months? Because I'm still shocked either of us came out alive. We get along better with distance, and you're better off in the dorms, believe me."

"Ugh. I know you're right," the girl says. "I just need to get off my ass and get a job. How's that Hooters gig working out for you?"

Bridgette scoffs. "It's the worst job I've ever had." She turns around to pick up her phone and her eyes meet mine. I don't even try to hide the fact that I was listening to her conversation. She glares at me as she picks up the phone and holds it to her mouth. "I'll call you later, Brandi." She ends her call and slaps her phone against the counter. "What's your problem?"

I shrug. "Nothing," I say, straightening up and walking toward the kitchen.

Don't look at her shorts, don't look at her shorts.

"I just didn't realize you were capable of normal human interaction."

Bridgette rolls her eyes and picks up the plate of food she just finished preparing. She begins walking toward her bedroom. "I can be pleasant to people who deserve it."

When she reaches her door, she turns around and faces me. "I need you to drop me off at work in an hour. My car's in the shop." She disappears into her bedroom.

I grimace, because for some reason the thought of taking her to work excites me, and my excitement disappoints me. I feel like I'm two different people right now. I'm a guy who finds his new roommate insanely attractive, but I'm also a guy who can't stand to be around his bitchy new roommate.

I'm also a guy who's about to do some heavy research into the porn industry, because I have to find that movie. *Have* to. It's all I'm gonna be able to think about until I see it with my own eyes.

•   •   •

"What's Bridgette's last name?" I ask Brennan. I've texted him five times in the last half hour, trying to figure it out, but he hasn't texted me back, so now I'm on the phone with him. I'm sure a little Google search of her name could help me find the title.

"Cox. Why?"

I laugh. "Bridgette Cox? Seriously?"

There's a pause on his end of the line. "What's so funny? And why do you need her last name?"

"No reason," I say. "Thanks."

I hang up the phone without giving him an explanation. The last thing Brennan needs to know is that his possible sister was in a porn film.

But *Cox*? That's way too easy.

I spend the next fifteen minutes googling her name, looking for anything porn-related. I come up empty-handed. She must have used a fake name.

I slam my laptop shut when my bedroom door swings open. "Let's go," she says.

I stand up and slip on my shoes. "Ever heard of knocking?" I ask as I follow her through the living room.

"Really, Warren? Coming from the guy who's walked in on me in the bathroom no less than three times in the past two weeks?"

"Ever heard of locking doors?" I say in response.

She doesn't reply as she makes her way outside. I grab my keys off the bar and follow her. I am curious as to why she never locks the doors when she's in the shower. My first thought leads me to believe that maybe she likes it when I walk in on her. Why else would she leave them unlocked?

Come to think of it, she also wears that damn uniform way longer than she needs to. She puts it on a good two hours before going to work and she leaves it on just as long when she gets home. Most people spend as little time as possible in their work clothes, but Bridgette seems to like flaunting her ass in my face.

I pause at the bottom of the stairs and watch as her ass makes its way toward my car.

Holy shit. I think Bridgette is into me.

She turns around after she tries to open the locked door. She looks at me expectantly and I'm still frozen at the bottom of the stairs, staring at her, my mouth agape.

Bridgette likes me.

"Unlock the car, Warren. Jesus."

I lift the key fob and point it at the car to unlock the doors. Bridgette slides into her seat and flips the visor down, fingering at her hair. A smile slowly spreads across my face as I make my way to the driver's side.

Bridgette wants me.

This is gonna be fun.

After I back the car out, I keep half of my focus on the road and half of it on her legs. She has one propped up on the dash and she keeps running her hand up and down her thigh. I can't tell if she's doing it in a seductive way or because she likes the sound of her fingernails scraping over her panty hose.

I have to adjust in my seat and swallow the lump in my throat, because we've never actually been this close before for this long. The tension is thick, and I can't tell if it's all mine or if it's a shared tension. I clear my throat and do what I can to not make this the most awkward ten miles I've ever had to drive.

"So," I say, attempting to think of something to break the ice. "Do you like your job?"

Bridgette laughs under her breath. "Yes, Warren. I *love* it. I love when disgusting old men grab my ass night after night, and I especially love it when drunk guys think my boobs are an accessory and not an extension of my body."

I shake my head. I don't know why I thought it would be a good idea to speak to her. I exhale and don't bother asking her any more questions. She's impossible to talk to.

Silence engulfs the car for another two miles. I hear her sigh heavily and I turn and glance at her, but she's staring out the window. "The tips are good," she says quietly.

I smile and look back at the road. I smile, because I know that's as close to an apology as Bridgette is capable of giving. "That's good," I say to her, my way of telling her I accept her apology.

We're quiet until we reach her work. I stop out front and she gets out of the car and then leans down and looks at me. "I need you to pick me up at eleven tonight."

She slams the door shut without saying please or thank you or goodbye. And even though she's the most inconsiderate person I've ever met in real life, I can't stop smiling.

I think we may have just bonded.

• • •

After I make it home, the first thing I do is set timers on every single porn on pay-per-view. I spend the next few hours fast-forwarding through most of them, pausing it any time it lands on a girl that even remotely resembles her. I take into account that she may have been wearing a wig, so I can't rule women out simply based on their hair color.

Ridge takes a seat next to me on the couch and I consider putting the TV on caption for him, but I don't. Let's be honest, pornos aren't known for their riveting story lines.

Ridge elbows me to get my attention. "What's with this new fascination?" he asks, referring to the fact that I've done nothing today other than watch porn after porn.

I don't want to be honest, so I just shrug. "I like porn."

He nods his head slowly and then stands up. "I'm not gonna lie," he signs. "It's really awkward. I'll be out on my balcony if you need me."

I pause the TV. "You worked out any new songs yet?"

Ridge looks frustrated when I ask him this. He shakes his head. "Not yet." He walks away and I feel bad for asking. I don't know what's changed over the last few months, but he's not the same. He seems more stressed out than usual, and it makes me wonder if he and Maggie have been fighting. He says they're fine, but he's never had a problem writing music for the band before, and everyone knows the number one source for musical inspiration comes from relationships.

Ridge and Brennan are both musically inclined and I've always been a little bit jealous in that regard. Granted, I'm jealous of Ridge in a lot of ways. He just seems to have been born with a certain level of maturity, and I've always envied that about him. He's not impulsive like I am and he also seems to take people's feelings into consideration more than I do. I know Brennan has always looked up to him and I definitely do, too, so seeing him struggling with whatever is going on in that head of his is tough. He knew what he was getting into when he began dating Maggie, so I'm not sure if he's growing unhappy in his relationship with her or if maybe he's concerned she's unhappy with him. Whatever it is, I'm not sure what I can do to help him.

I don't think I *can* help him.

I give my focus back to the TV and fast-forward through at least three more films before I realize it's already eleven and I'm late picking up Bridgette.

Shit. Time flies when you're watching porn.

I spend the next several minutes in fast-forward, making it the ten miles to Hooters in record time. When I pull up, she's standing outside with her arms folded across her chest, shooting daggers at my car. She swings the door open and climbs in. "You're late."

I wait until she slams the door before pressing on the gas. "You're welcome for the ride, Bridgette."

I can feel the anger radiating from her. I don't know if it's simply because I'm late picking her up or because she had a shitty night at work, but I'm not about to ask. When we pull into the complex, she jumps out of my car before I even have it in park. She stalks up the stairs and slams the front door shut.

When I reach the apartment, she's already in her bedroom. I try to be understanding, but this is just . . . *it's fucking rude.* I give her a ride to and from work and all she does is bitch at me? You don't have to be taught manners to know how inappropriate that kind of behavior is. Hell, I'm one of the most inconsiderate people I know, and I would never treat someone like she's treating me.

I walk to my bedroom and head straight for the bathroom. She's already in there, standing at the sink, washing her face. "Again with the failure to knock?" she says with a dramatic roll of her eyes.

I ignore her and walk to the toilet. I lift the lid and unzip my pants. I try to keep my smile in check when I hear her scoff at the fact that I just started taking a piss with her in the bathroom.

"Are you serious?"

I continue to ignore her comments and flush the toilet when I'm finished. I leave the lid up on purpose and step over to the sink, right next to her. *Two can play at this asshole game, Bridgette.*

I grab my toothbrush and squirt toothpaste on it and then start brushing my teeth. She elbows me when I get in the way of the sink, attempting to push me aside. I elbow her right back and continue brushing. I look up at our reflection in the mirror and like what I see. I'm several inches taller than her. My hair is darker than hers, and my eyes are brown compared to her greens. We complement each other, though. Standing next to each other like this, I can see how we could make a good-looking couple. We'd probably even make some good-looking children.

Shit.

Why am I allowing thoughts like this to fester in my brain?

She finishes wiping the makeup from her face before grabbing her own toothbrush. Now we're both fighting for sink space, brushing with more force than our teeth have probably ever been brushed. We take turns angrily spitting into the sink, throwing elbows at each other between every turn.

When I'm finished, I rinse off my toothbrush and put it back in the holder. She does the same. I cup my hands under the stream of water and bend forward to take a sip when she shoves me aside, causing me to splash water all over the counter. I wait until she has water in her own hands, then I shove her arms, watching the water splash everywhere.

She grips the counter and takes a deep, calming breath. It doesn't help, though, because she splashes her hand through the faucet stream, sending a handful of water straight at my face.

I close my eyes and try to put myself in her shoes. Maybe she's had a rough day. Maybe she hates her job. Maybe she hates her life.

Whatever her reason for acting the way she does doesn't excuse the fact that she still didn't say thank you for the ride. She's treating me like I ruined her life, and all I've done is try to accommodate her.

I open my eyes and don't even look at her. I reach over, turn the sink faucet off, and then grab the hand towel and begin drying my face. She's watching me closely, waiting for me to retaliate. I take a slow step toward her, towering over her. She presses her back against the sink and keeps her eyes focused on mine as I lean forward.

Our chests are almost touching now. I can feel the heat radiating from her as her lips slowly part. She's not pushing me away this time. In fact, it looks like she's daring me to keep going. To come closer.

I place my hands on either side of her, locking her in. She still doesn't resist and I know if I tried to kiss her right now, she wouldn't resist that, either. Under any other circumstance, I *would* be kissing her right now. My tongue would be as far into that mouth as I could get it, because *fuck it's a nice mouth.* I don't know how so much venom can spew from lips as soft as hers.

"Bridgette," I say, very calmly.

I can see the roll of her throat as she swallows, still looking up at me. "Warren," she says, her voice a mix between resolved and desperate.

I smile at her, just inches from her face. The fact that she's allowing me this close only proves that my theory earlier this afternoon is correct. She wants me. She wants me to touch her, to kiss her, to carry her to my bed. I wonder if she's as mean in the bedroom as she is out of the bedroom.

I lean in another inch and she gasps quietly, trading glances between my eyes and my lips. I pull my bottom lip into my mouth, slowly sliding my teeth across it. She watches my mouth with fascination. My heart is in my throat and my palms are sweating, because I'm not sure I can do this. I'm not so sure I can resist her.

I lean in even closer, reaching around her with my right hand until I find the mouthwash on the counter. Just when our lips would meet if I were to kiss her, I pull back and step away, removing the lid from the mouthwash. I keep my eyes focused on hers and take a sip before putting the lid back on it and setting it down on the counter.

I can see the desire in her eyes become swallowed up by fury. She's pissed at me, pissed at herself. Possibly even embarrassed. When she sees I was teasing her, the corners of her eyes crinkle with her intense glare. I step up to the sink and spit the mouthwash out, wiping my mouth with the hand towel again. I turn toward my bedroom. "Goodnight, Bridgette."

I close the door and lean against it and squeeze my eyes shut. Her bedroom door slams shut and I blow out a steady breath. I've never been more turned on than I am right now. I've also never been more proud of myself than I am right now. Walking away from that mouth and those hungry eyes was the hardest thing I've had to do, but also the most important. I have to keep the upper hand, because that girl has way too much power over me, and she doesn't even know it.

I turn out my bedroom light and walk to my bed, trying to get the image of what almost just happened out of my head. After several minutes, I give up trying to fight it. I decide to use the thoughts of her to my advantage as I slip my hand into my boxers, thinking about those orange shorts. That mouth. The small gasp of breath she took when I leaned in toward her.

I close my eyes and think about what could have happened if I wasn't so stubborn. If I would have just kissed her. I also think about the fact that she's just a few feet away, hopefully just as sexually frustrated as I am right now.

Why does she have to be so damn mean? Mean girls are my weakness, and I think I just now figured that out.

Chapter Five

It's been three days since our moment in the bathroom. I've noticed she keeps the doors locked now, which is fine. I'm sure she's pissed off that she allowed herself to have a moment of weakness. She doesn't seem like the type to give in as easily as she almost did.

Either way, I can't decide if I made the right move. Half of me rejoices in the fact that I was able to walk away, but the other half of me can't believe how stupid I was for passing up an opportunity like that. I could have had her, and now I more than likely won't ever. But it's for the best, because the last thing I need is to hook up with a roommate who could potentially be the sister of my best friend. But she makes it hard, pun intended, when she walks into the living room looking like she does right now. She's not in her work clothes, but what she does have on doesn't make it any better. She's wearing a thin tank top over a barely there pair of pajama shorts, and she's walked between me and the TV more times than I can count.

Shit.

Now she's heading toward me with books in her hands.

Shit.

She's sitting on the couch. Next to me. In that thin tank top. Without a bra.

I can handle this. I force my eyes on the TV, still in

search of whatever porn she was in. I could just ask her, but that's not a good idea. If she knows I know she was in a porn film, she'd probably do everything she could to make sure I never find out.

She leans forward and picks up the remote, and then points it at the TV to mute it. I don't know who she thinks she is, but if she doesn't want to hear the TV, she can go to her room. I grab the remote and turn the sound back on. She sighs and opens one of her textbooks and begins reading.

I pretend I'm paying attention to the TV, but I can't stop stealing glances at her, because *holy shit, I can't believe I walked away from her.* I'm an idiot.

She grabs the remote and mutes the TV again, possibly because one of the girls was screaming at the top of her lungs. I wonder if Bridgette is loud during sex? Probably not. She's more than likely stubborn, refusing to give up any of her sounds.

I unmute the TV again and she reaches her breaking point. "I'm trying to study, Warren. For fuck's sake, you still get the same effect when it's on mute."

I eye her curiously. "How would you know? Are you a porn expert?"

She glances at me, a flash of suspicion in her eyes. "Can you please, for one night, forgo your addiction so I can study in peace and quiet?"

Bridgette said "please."

"Go study in your bedroom," I say.

Her mouth presses into a tight, thin line. She pushes her book off her lap and stands. She walks toward the TV and reaches behind it, pulling the plug. After returning to the couch, she pulls her book back onto her lap and resumes studying.

I don't know how I ever got beyond her horrible attitude enough to even be attracted to her. She's vile. I don't care how good she looks, she'll never find anyone who can put up with her personality.

"You can be a real bitch sometimes, you know that?"

She releases an exasperated breath. "Yeah, well. You're addicted to porn."

I laugh under my breath. "At least I wasn't *in* a porn."

Her eyes swing in my direction. "I knew you were eavesdropping."

I shrug. "I couldn't help it. You were having a conversation like you were an actual human being. It was fascinating."

Her focus falls back onto the pages of the textbook. "You're an asshole."

"You're an opportunist."

She slams her book shut and turns to face me on the couch. "An opportunist? Are you kidding me?"

I pull my knee up and turn and face her. "You don't think it seems a little fishy that you show up out of the blue and claim to be the long-lost sister to the most popular local band in Austin?"

She looks capable of murder. "Warren, I suggest you stop making accusations against people you know absolutely nothing about."

I grin, because I know that got to her. I might come out victorious again.

"I've learned enough about you to know you don't deserve to be trusted." I pick up her book and put it back in her lap and point to her bedroom. "Now take your homework and go back to your borrowed room."

"*My* borrowed room? You don't even pay rent, Warren."

"Neither do you, Bridgette."

"All you do is watch porn and stare at my ass. You're a lazy pervert."

"All you do is *flaunt* your ass and fantasize about me kissing you."

"You're disgusting," she says. "As a matter of fact, *watch* the porn. I'm sure you need all the pointers you can get."

Okay, that's low. She can insult my laziness, my finances, my new porn addiction, but she cannot insult my bedroom skills. Especially when she doesn't have firsthand experience. "I don't need pointers to please a woman, Bridgette. I was born with natural talent."

She's eyeing me like she's about to punch me, but I can't stop staring at her mouth, hoping she insults me again. Somewhere between being called an asshole and this moment, I've become more turned on than I've ever been in my life. I'm hoping she's about to storm off to her bedroom because I've already met my quota for restraint when it comes to her.

She licks her bottom lip, and I have to grip the couch cushion to keep myself from attacking that mouth. Her eyes are focused intensely on mine, and we're both breathing so heavily from our verbal attacks, I can taste her breath on my lips.

"I hate you," she says through clenched teeth.

"I hated you first," I hiss back.

Her focus falls on my mouth and as soon as I see the tiniest flash of desire in her eyes, I lunge forward. I grab her face and press my lips to hers as I shove her back against the couch. She's pushing me away with her knees while pulling me to her with her hands. My tongue forces through the barrier of her lips and she devours me in response. I kiss her hard, and she kisses me even harder. I'm pulling at a fistful of her hair while she scratches down my neck with her fingernails. *Fuck*, it hurts. *She* hurts.

I want more.

I'm hovering over her and then pressing myself against her, pulling her knee up so she can wrap it around my waist. Her hands are in my hair, and I don't want her to move out. I want her to stay. I want her to be my roommate forever. She's the best fucking roommate I've ever had and, my God, she's so *nice.* How did I ever think she was mean? She's so, so sweet, and her lips are sweet and *Bridgette, I love your name.*

"Bridgette," I whisper, wanting to say her name out loud. I don't know how I hated her name before this moment, because it's the most beautiful name I've ever said out loud.

I pull away from her mouth and begin working my way down her sweet, sweet neck. As soon as I make it to her shoulder, she begins to push me away with her hands.

Just like that, I snap back to reality and separate from her willingly.

I move to the other end of the couch, needing the space to wrap my head around *what the hell just happened?*

She quickly sits up on the couch. She wipes her mouth and I run my hands through my hair, doing whatever I can to process this.

She's an evil vixen. I close my eyes and squeeze my forehead, trying to figure out how I just lost complete control of myself simply because I was kissing her. I think of all the lies that were just passing through my head as my dick tried to convince me she was actually a decent person.

I'm weak. I'm so weak, and she just gained the upper hand again.

"Don't do that again," she says, angry and breathless.

Her voice makes me wince. "You started it," I say defensively.

Did she? I can't remember. It might have been mutual.

"You kiss like you're trying to resuscitate a dead cat," she says, disgusted.

"You kiss like you *are* a dead cat."

She pulls her knees up to her chest and wraps her arms around them. She looks extremely uncomfortable in the silence, so it doesn't surprise me when she spits out another insult. "You probably fuck like a limp noodle."

"I fuck like I'm Thor."

I'm not looking at her, but I know that comment had to make her smile. If she's even capable of smiling. The silence grows heavier and neither of us moves, making it even more apparent that what just happened was a mistake.

"Why do you taste like onions?" she asks.

I shrug. "I just ate pizza."

She glances into the kitchen. "Is there any left?"

I nod. "It's in the fridge."

She immediately stands up to walk to the kitchen, and I hate that I'm staring at her shirt. I can see her nipples poking through the thin fabric, and I want to point at her and say, *"I did that! That's all me!"*

Instead, I close my eyes and try to think about whatever

will stop my wanting to follow her into that kitchen and bend her over the counter. Luckily, Ridge's bedroom door opens, so I give my full attention to him as he walks into the living room. He pauses when he sees me sitting on the couch. He glances at the TV that isn't even on. "Why do you look so guilty?"

I shake my head shamefully. "I think I just made out with Bridgette," I sign.

Ridge looks at Bridgette, who is standing in the kitchen with her back to us. He shakes his head in disappointment. Or confusion.

"Why?" he asks, perplexed. "Did she do it willingly?"

I grab one of the couch pillows and throw it at him. "Yes, she did it willingly, asshole. She wants me."

"Do you want her?" He seems genuinely shocked, like he didn't see this coming at all.

I shake my head. "No, I don't want her," I sign. "But I feel like I need her. So bad. She's so . . ." I pause my hands for a few seconds before continuing. "She's the best worst thing that's ever happened to me."

Ridge backs up until his hand is on the front door. "I'm going to Maggie's for the night," he signs. "We'll pray for you."

I flip him off as he makes his way out. When I turn back to face Bridgette, she's walking toward her bedroom. She passes the TV and doesn't even have the audacity to plug it back in.

I plug in the TV, because there isn't a doubt in my mind now. I *have* to find that porno, because after experiencing that kiss, I'm addicted. Addicted to all things Bridgette.

·   ·   ·

I barely slept last night. Being in the same apartment with her, knowing Ridge and Brennan were both gone, was too much. It took all I had not to make an excuse to knock on her bedroom door. But I'm learning how her mind works, and I know she'd turn me down in a heartbeat just to stay in control.

And now, Ridge and Brennan are both still gone and she's at work and I've exhausted all the porn on pay-per-view. I can't keep track of how much porn I've watched in the past two weeks. It's ridiculous. How many could there possibly be? And I've narrowed it down to the ones that have been recorded in the last few years, because she had to be over eighteen when she filmed it. She's twenty-two now, so that's four years of porn films to sift through.

Oh, my God. I'm obsessed.

I'm like a stalker.

I *am* a stalker.

The front door swings open and Bridgette walks in. She slams it shut so hard, I flinch. She walks to the kitchen and begins opening cabinets and banging them shut. She finally rests her palms on the bar and looks straight at me. "Where the hell do you keep the alcohol?"

Bad day, I guess.

I stand up and walk over to the sink. I open the cabinet beneath it and take out the bottle of Pine-Sol. I don't even bother grabbing her a glass. She looks like the type who can take a good swig.

"Are you trying to kill me?" she asks, staring at the bottle in my hands.

I push it into her hand. "Ridge thinks he's clever by hiding it in old cleaner bottles. He doesn't like it when I drink all his alcohol."

She brings the bottle to her nose and winces. "Is whiskey the only thing you have?"

I nod. She shrugs and brings the bottle to her lips, tilts her head back, and takes a long swig.

She hands the bottle back to me as she wipes her mouth with the back of her hand. I take a sip from the bottle myself and then hand it back to her. We do this several times until her anger seems to have subsided, as much as anger can subside in Bridgette's world. I put the top back on the bottle and return it to the cabinet.

"Bad day?" I ask.

She leans against the counter and pulls at the elastic of her orange shorts. "The worst."

"Want to talk about it?"

She looks up at me through her lashes and then rolls her eyes. "No," she says flatly.

I don't push it. I don't even know that I really want to know about her day. Anything and everything seems to set her off, so she's probably pissed over something stupid, like a red light on her way home. It has to be exhausting to respond to all aspects of life with so much anger.

"Why are you always so mad?"

She laughs under her breath. "That's easy," she says. "Assholes, stupid customers, a shitty job, worthless parents, crappy friends, bad weather, annoying roommates who don't know how to kiss."

I laugh at the last comment, which I'm sure was supposed to be a dig, but it felt more like an underhanded flirt.

"How are you so happy all the time?" she asks. "You think everything is funny."

"That's easy," I say. "Great parents, being lucky enough to have a job, loyal friends, sunny days, and roommates who starred in porn films."

She glances away quickly in an attempt to hide a smile that almost appeared on her face. God, I wish she would let that smile out, because I'm dying to see what it looks like. As long as she's lived here, I'm not sure that I've ever seen her smile.

"Is that why you watch so much porn? Because you're hoping to find out which one I was in?"

I don't nod, but I don't shake my head, either. I lean my hip into the counter and fold my arms over my chest. "Just tell me the name of it."

"No," she says quickly. "Besides, I was just an extra. I didn't even really do anything."

An extra. That helps narrow down my search a little.

"*Didn't really* do anything doesn't mean *didn't*."

She rolls her eyes at me, but she's still standing here, so I keep going. "Were you naked?"

"It was a porn, Warren. I wasn't wearing a sweater."

That means yes.

"Did you have sex on camera?"

She shakes her head. "No."

"But you made out with a guy?"

She shakes her head again. "Wasn't a guy."

Holy fuck.

I turn around and grip the bar with one hand while

making the form of a cross over my body with the other. When I turn back around, she's still standing in the same spot, but she actually looks relaxed. She should drink whiskey every day.

"So you're telling me you made out with another girl? And it's documented somewhere? On film?"

The corner of her mouth curls up into a ghostly smile.

"You smiled."

She stops smiling immediately. "I did not."

I take a step toward her and nod my head. "Yes, you did. I made you smile."

She begins to shake her head in disagreement, so I slip my hand behind her neck. Her eyes widen, and I'm almost positive she's about to push me away, but I can't help it. *That smile*.

"You *did* smile, Bridgette," I whisper. "And you need to own it, because it was fucking beautiful."

She gasps in shock right before my lips crash against hers. I don't think she was expecting this kiss to happen, but she certainly isn't objecting. Her mouth is warm and responsive and when I part her lips with my tongue, she actually lets me.

I don't know if it's the whiskey or her, but my heart is thrashing around in my chest like a caged beast. I slide my hands down her back until they meet her ass and I squeeze as I pick her up and set her back down on the bar.

Our lips separate, and we stare at each other silently, each of us hesitant to believe that the other isn't about to walk away again. When I realize that neither of us seems to want to stop this, I bring my hands up to her cheeks and lean in again, taking her lips between mine.

This is different from our kiss the other night. Our first kiss was quick and frantic, because we knew that's where it would end.

This one is slow and deep, and feels like it's just the beginning of what we're about to experience tonight. This time when I leave her mouth to taste her neck, she doesn't push me away. She pulls me closer, wanting me to kiss her harder.

"Warren," she whispers, tilting her neck to the side, allowing me free rein of her skin. "If I have sex with you, you have to promise you won't get clingy afterward."

I laugh, but I don't move away from her neck. "If you have sex with me, Bridgette, *you're* the one in danger of becoming clingy. You'll want so much more of me, I won't be able to tell the difference between you and Saran Wrap."

She laughs, and I pull away from her. I look down at her mouth and then into her eyes. *"My God."*

She shakes her head, confused. "What?"

"Your laugh." I kiss her on the lips. "Fucking phenomenal," I whisper into her mouth. I lift her off the counter and keep her wrapped around me as I make my way across the living room. As soon as we're in my bedroom, I close the door and push her against it. I keep her pressed against the door with my body while I remove my shirt. I find the hem of her shirt and begin to pull it over her head. "I can't tell you how many times I've fantasized about this, Bridgette."

She helps me pull her shirt over her head. "I haven't fantasized about it at all," she says.

I smile. "Bullshit."

I lift her again and carry her to the bed. As soon as I lay her on it and begin to crawl on top of her, she pushes my shoulders and shoves me onto my back. Her hands meet the button on my jeans and she undoes them. I attempt to take control again by pushing her onto her back, but she's not having it. She straddles me and places her hands on my biceps, pushing my arms against the bed. "I make the calls," she says.

I don't argue. If she wants to be in charge, I'll absolutely let her.

She sits up straight and brings her hands around to her back to undo her bra. I lift up and begin to reach around to assist her, but her hands are back on my arms in a flash. She pushes me to the mattress again. "What did I just say, Warren?"

Holy shit. She's not kidding.

I nod and focus my attention back to her bra as she lifts up and unfastens it. She slides the straps slowly down her arms and I can't keep my eyes off her. I want to touch her, to help her, to be the one to remove her bra, but she's not allowing me to do anything.

My breath catches in my chest when she flings the bra away.

My God, she's perfect. Her breasts are the perfect size, appearing as if they would fit right in the palms of my hands. But I wouldn't know, because I'm not allowed to touch them.

Am I?

I hesitantly lift my hands to feel the softness of her skin, but she immediately shoves my arms away from her, back to the bed.

God, it's torture. Her breasts are *right here*, inches from me, and I can't even touch them.

"Where are your condoms?"

I point to the nightstand on the opposite side of the bed. She slides off me and I watch her closely as she walks to my nightstand. She opens the drawer and sifts around until she finds one. She puts it between her teeth as she walks back toward the foot of the bed. She doesn't climb back on top of me. Instead, she hooks her thumbs into the waistband of her shorts and begins to shimmy out of them.

I'm harder than I've ever been, and I can feel my pulse throbbing throughout my whole body. She needs to hurry the hell up and climb back on top of me.

She leaves her panties on as she bends over and begins to pull my jeans the rest of the way off. She hooks her hands in my underwear and pulls them down as well, the condom wrapper still dangling between her teeth. Her hair is the perfect length, trailing lightly over my skin like feathers every time she leans over me.

Once all my clothes are off, her eyes focus on the hardest part of me. A smile tugs at her lips and her eyes meet mine. She pulls the condom out of her mouth.

"Impressive," she says. "This definitely explains your inflated ego."

I take the insult with the compliment, because I already know Bridgette isn't the type to dish them out.

She straddles me again, still wearing her panties. She leans forward and presses her palms into my forearms. Her mouth meets mine, and her breasts press against my chest, causing me to groan. She feels incredible. So good. I'm worried now, because we haven't even had sex yet and I can already tell I'm ruined.

I can feel her wetness through her panties as she torturously slides up and down, up and down, as slow as she possibly can. Her tongue is in my mouth, and I keep trying to grab the back of her head, or grip her by the waist, but every time I move, she stops me.

I imagined she would be bossy in the bedroom, but nothing like this. She won't even let me touch her, and it's fucking killing me.

"Open your mouth," she whispers into my ear. I do, and she places the condom wrapper between my teeth. I bite down on it and she uses her own teeth to grip the other end of it as she pulls away from me, tearing the wrapper open between both our mouths.

Okay, that was hot.

So hot.

We should quit our jobs and do this full-time.

She pulls out the condom and sits straight up. She looks down and licks her lips as she slides the condom over me and I moan, because her hands are *fuck. They're too much. I want them everywhere.*

I understand how guys can say stupid shit in the throes of passion, because I want to say so much to her right now. I want to tell her I love her and that we're soul mates and that she should marry me, because her hands make me think stupid, stupid, untrue thoughts like this.

She lifts up higher on her knees and pulls her panties to the side, leaving them on as she begins to lower herself on top of me.

It's official. She's the best roommate I've ever had in my life.

She winces slightly when she begins to take me inside

her, and I feel kind of bad that it hurts her. But not bad enough to stop myself from lifting my hips and sliding into her the rest of the way.

As soon as we're flush together, we moan in unison.

I've never felt anything like it.

It's as if her body contours perfectly to mine, fitting every line and curve and dip. Neither of us moves an inch while we fill the room with heavy gasps, giving ourselves a moment to adjust to the sheer perfection we just created.

"Fuck," I whisper.

"Okay," she replies.

She begins to move, and I don't know what to do with myself. My hands want to hold her by the waist as she slides up and down, but I also know I'm not allowed to touch her. My eyes take her in as she continues her movements, her perfect, methodical, sweet movements.

After several minutes of watching her on top of me with her eyes closed and her lips parted, I give up. I can't not touch her. My hands grip her waist and she tries to pull them away but I just grip harder, lifting her when she rises and pulling her down when she falls. She gives up trying to fight me after seeing how much better my strength can make it feel.

I want to hear her moan and I want to hear her fall apart on top of me, but she's holding it all back, just like I knew she would.

I slide my hands up her back and pull her forward until our mouths meet. I keep one hand on the back of her head and one on her waist as she continues her rhythm on top of me.

I curve my hand around her hip and slowly slide it over her stomach, until I'm touching her. I slide a finger between us, separating her, feeling her warmth and wetness surround me. She moans into my mouth and I begin to rub her, but she immediately stops moving. She grabs my wrist and pulls it away from her, slapping my arm against the mattress again.

Her eyes open and focus firmly on mine as she slowly begins to move again. "Keep your hands on the mattress, Warren," she warns.

Dammit, she's making this difficult. I need to feel her again, and when I'm done touching her, I want to taste her. I want that wetness and warmth all over my tongue.

But first, I'll let her have her way. I close my eyes and stop trying to take control. I focus on her tightness, swallowing me up. I focus on the fact that each time her body meets mine, I'm as deep inside her as I can possibly go.

She leans forward and her breasts dance back and forth across my chest as she moves on top of me.

Heaven is *definitely* for real.

My legs begin to tense and my hands are searching for something to grip as I feel myself building. She can sense I'm near release, so she tightens around me and her thrusts become faster and harder. I keep my eyes closed as my body begins to shake beneath her.

I want to cuss and groan, and let her know how good this feels as I release inside of her, but I don't make a single noise. If I'm not allowed to touch her while I come, then she's not allowed to hear how much I fucking love every second of it.

She continues to move over me as I quietly succumb to the tremors. When it's over, she comes to a stop on top of me. I open my eyes and look up at her and catch her smiling down at me. As soon as she realizes I'm looking at her, the smile is gone.

I want her to collapse against my chest. I want to roll her onto her back and take her in my mouth until she's screaming my name out in ecstasy, rather than anger.

Instead, she slowly slides off of me. She stands and turns toward the bathroom. "Goodnight, Warren."

The door closes behind her and I'm lying here in complete confusion. I would be running after her right about now, but I'm still too weak to move.

I give myself time to regroup, and then I remove the condom and toss it into the bathroom trash can on my way to her bedroom. I swing open the door just as she's crawling into her bed. As soon as her head meets her pillow, I'm on top of her, kissing her. As expected, she pushes me away.

"What did I say about being clingy?" she says, pulling her face from mine.

"I'm not being clingy," I say, kissing my way down her neck. "We're not finished."

She pulls away even farther and pushes my face back. "I'm pretty sure we finished, Warren. About three minutes ago."

"*I* finished," I say, looking her in the eyes. "But *you* didn't finish." I can feel her resistance as she attempts to roll over.

"Warren, stop," she says, pushing me away.

I don't pull away from her. Instead, I wrap my arm around her and slowly move my hand across her stomach.

That's when she slaps me.

I immediately pull back and look down at her in shock.

She pushes me away and scoots up on her bed until her

back meets the headboard. "I said stop," she says, defending her slap.

I work my jaw back and forth, not sure what to do. In all my years of experience with girls and even in all the recent porn I've been watching, this isn't how sex usually goes. People are selfish by nature and the fact that she doesn't even want me to get her off is confusing the hell out of me.

"Am I . . ." I pause and look at her. "Am I misreading something here? Because I thought . . ."

"We fucked, Warren. It's over, now go to sleep."

I shake my head. "No, Bridgette. *You* fucked. *You* did all the work and you didn't even get to enjoy it. I don't understand why you won't let me touch you."

She groans, frustrated. "Warren, it's fine. It was fun." She looks away from me. "I just don't like the other part, so go to bed."

She doesn't like the other part? The part where she has an amazing, mind-blowing orgasm?

"Okay," I say. "I'll go to bed."

"Thank you," she mutters.

"But first," I say, holding up my finger. "I need to know something."

She rolls her eyes. "What?"

I lean toward her and look at her with fascination. "Is this how sex *always* is with you? You have to be in complete control, to the point where you don't even allow someone to get you off?"

She kicks at me with her foot, trying to get me to leave her bed. "I'm not discussing my sex life with you, Warren. Go back to your room."

She scoots down on her bed until her head meets her pillow. She rolls over until her back is to me and she pulls the covers up over her head.

Holy shit. This is . . . I don't even know what to think. I've never met anyone like her. She has some serious control issues.

"Bridgette," I whisper, needing her to roll over and talk to me again. She ignores me, but I can't leave because this conversation needs to happen. "Are you telling me you've never had an orgasm during sex?"

The covers fly off her head and she rolls onto her back. "It's never been an issue with anyone until you," she says angrily.

I laugh and shake my head and for some reason, feel extremely happy about this. Because she's apparently been with some really selfish assholes in the past, and I'm about to show her what she's been missing.

She pulls the covers back over her head and faces the opposite direction again. Rather than stand and walk back to my room like I know she wants me to do, I lift the covers and slide in behind her. I wrap my arm over her, pressing my palm against her stomach, pulling her against my chest.

She practically growls at me. "Warren, *stop*. Believe it or not, I'm perfectly happy with my sex life, and I don't need you to *Oh, my God*." She stops mid-rant as soon as I cup her between the legs.

I rest my cheek against hers. "I need you to shut up, Bridgette."

She doesn't move, so I roll her onto her stomach and slide on top of her. I pin her arms beneath my hands, just like she did me earlier. "Please don't resist me," I whisper into her ear. "I want to be in control, and I want you to do what I say." I run my tongue across her ear and watch as the chills break out on her neck. "Understood?"

Her breaths are shallow, and she squeezes her eyes shut with her nod.

"Thank you," I tell her. I kiss my way down her neck and shoulder, and then work my kisses slowly across her back. Her entire body is tense and knowing that she's never experienced an orgasm at the hands of another guy already has me hard again.

I reach down to her thighs and spread her legs with my hand. She buries her face into her pillow and it makes me smile. She's never been this vulnerable with someone else, and she doesn't want to give me the pleasure of seeing how much she enjoys it.

I keep my eyes focused on her anyway as I slowly push two fingers inside of her, waiting for her to moan into her pillow.

She doesn't make a sound, so I pull them out and re-enter her with three fingers this time.

I press my forehead into her pillow, right next to her face, and I wait for the sounds to escape.

Nothing. I laugh quietly, because I really have my work cut out for me.

I pull my hand away from her and flip her onto her back. Her eyes are still closed tightly so I grab her jaw and press my lips to hers. I kiss her hard and deep, until she begins to kiss me back with just as much anger. She pulls at my hair and spreads her legs for me, wanting me to bury myself inside of her.

I do. I push her panties aside and shove into her so hard and fast, she lets out a moan and *my God, I need more of that. So much more.* But I don't have on a condom, and this time isn't about me, so I pull out of her. I take one of her breasts in my hands and bring it to my mouth.

I slowly kiss my way down her stomach, and the lower I get, the tenser her body grows. I can feel her hesitation, and part of me wants to devour her immediately, but part of me needs to know that I'm not going too far, too fast. I can tell by the stiffness in her posture that she's nervous now. I position both my hands on her waist and look up at her. She's chewing nervously on her bottom lip and her eyes are terrified.

"Have you never let anyone do this to you?" I whisper.

She releases her bottom lip with the shake of her head. "I don't like it."

"How would you know?"

She shrugs. "I just know."

I pull her hips down several inches on the bed. "You're too stubborn for your own good." I lift her and begin to lower my mouth to her, but she pulls back and sits up.

"Don't. I don't want to do this."

I grip her hips and pull her back down. "Lie back and close your eyes, Bridgette."

She continues to look at me with fear in her eyes, refusing to lie back down, so I lift up onto the palms of my hands. "Will you please stop being so stubborn and just relax? *Fuck*, woman. I want to give you the best ten minutes you've ever had in your life, but you're making it really difficult."

She bites her lip hesitantly, but she does as I say and slowly lowers herself to the bed, relaxing into her pillow.

I smile triumphantly and press my lips to her stomach again. I start just below her belly button and trail slow kisses all the way down until I meet her panties. I hook my fingers into the waistband and pull them down, over her hips, over her thighs, and I continue to slowly remove them until I'm at her ankles. Once I toss them on the floor, I lift her leg and press a soft kiss against her ankle, then her calf, then the inside of her knee, repeating the kisses all the way up her thigh, until I'm inches from sliding my tongue against her. As soon as I position my mouth over her, I can feel her warmth beckoning me.

"Warren, please . . ." she begins to protest. As soon as the word *please* leaves her mouth, my tongue slides against her, separating her. She lifts her hips several inches off the bed and cries out, so I grip her waist and pull her back down to the bed.

She's sweet and salty, and as soon as my mouth is against her, I'm convinced she could satiate every ounce of hunger I'll feel for the rest of my life.

She cries out again, still trying to pull away from me. "What . . . God . . . Warren . . ."

I continue to lick her, devour her, run my tongue over every bare part of her so that I leave no inch of her untasted. Her hands find their way back to my hair just as my fingers find their way back inside of her. I'm filling her, consuming her with my tongue, and she's taking every ounce of me she can get. She's no longer trying to scoot away from me. Now she's pressing my face into her, begging me to go faster.

Her hands leave my hair and meet her headboard as she grips it tightly and locks her legs around my shoulders. I keep my fingers buried inside of her as she cries out my name with each tremor that racks her body. I continue to please her until her shudders subside and her moans fade into silence.

I kiss the inside of her thigh as I pull my fingers out of her. I kiss all the way up her stomach until I'm pressed against her again, wanting to slide inside of her and stay the night.

I want to kiss her, but I don't know if she'd want that. Some girls prefer not to be kissed afterward, but my mouth is aching with a need to feel her lips against mine.

Apparently she wants the same thing, because she doesn't even hesitate when she pulls my face to hers and kisses me with a moan. There's so much pressure in every inch of my body, because I want to take her again. The only thing that can relieve that pressure is to push into her, which is exactly what I do.

She lifts her hips and meets my thrusts and I know I should stop. I have to stop.

I don't know why I can't stop.

I've never been inside a girl without a condom before, but she makes me stupid. She renders my conscience useless, and all I can think about is how incredible she feels.

And also how much I need to stop.

Stop, Warren. Stop.

I somehow pull out of her and press my face against her chest, gasping for air.

It hurts. God, it hurts. I live in the next room, where there's a drawer full of condoms, but I'm not sure I'd make it that far if I tried to stand.

She pulls my face back to hers and presses her lips to mine. She slides her hands down to my lower back and she pulls me against her, pressing her warmth against me as she urges me to move with her.

She feels incredible. It's not the same as being inside her, but the way she's moving against me feels pretty damn close. I close my eyes and bury my face against her neck as I work to increase the pace between us.

I grab a fistful of her hair and tilt her face to mine as I look down on her, watching as we both grow nearer to yet another release. She winces and I feel the first of her shudders pass through her. "Warren," she whispers. "Kiss me."

I do.

I cover her mouth with mine and drown out her moans with my own as I feel the warmth of my release spread between us. I'm holding her as tight as I can, kissing her as hard as I can.

All my weight is against her now that I'm physically incapable of holding myself up for another second. Her hands slide from my neck and fall to the bed. I'm too weak to speak, or I would be telling her how amazing she is. How good she feels. How perfect her body is and how she just single-handedly got the upper hand for all of eternity.

I can't speak, though. My eyes fall shut from pure exhaustion.

Pure, blissful exhaustion.

•   •   •

"Warren."

I try to open my eyes, but I can't. Or I just don't want to. I don't think I've ever experienced as deep of a sleep as the one I'm being torn from right now.

Her hand is on my shoulder and she's shaking me. I lift my head and turn to face her, curious if she's ready for another round. I smile at her through sleepy eyes.

"Go to your room," she says, kicking me with her feet. "You're snoring."

My eyes fall shut again but they fly open when her cold feet meet my stomach. She uses the strength of her legs to try and push me out of her bed. *"Go,"* she groans. "I can't sleep."

I somehow push myself into a standing position. I look down at her and she rolls onto her stomach, flips her pillow over, and sprawls out across her mattress.

I shuffle my way across her bedroom, through our bathroom and to my own bed. I fall onto it and close my eyes, taking all of three seconds to fall right back to sleep.

Chapter Six

I'm convinced that I've never slept as well as I did last night. And even though she kicked me out of her bed, I still feel victorious. Like royalty.

After I'm showered and dressed, I join Ridge in the kitchen. He's cleaning up what looks like breakfast, which is odd, because neither of us ever cooks breakfast. But then I understand when Maggie emerges from his room.

"Morning, Maggie," I say to her with a smile.

She eyes me cautiously. "What's with you?"

Right at that moment, Bridgette's bedroom door opens. We all watch her walk into the living room. She pauses when she looks up and sees us all staring at her.

"Morning, Bridgette," I say with a triumphant smile. "Sleep well?"

She sees the look on my face and immediately rolls her eyes. "Screw you, Warren." She walks into the kitchen and begins rummaging through the refrigerator, searching for something to eat. I watch her the entire time, until Ridge taps me on the shoulder.

"You had sex with her?" he signs.

I immediately shake my head in defense. "No," I sign back. "Maybe. I don't know. It was an accident."

Maggie and Ridge both laugh. He grabs Maggie's hand and pulls her toward his bedroom. "Come on," he signs. "I don't want to be in here when Bridgette realizes her mistake."

I watch them retreat back to Ridge's room, and then I turn and face Bridgette. She's glaring at me.

"Did you just tell him we had sex?"

I find myself once again shaking my head. "He already knew. I told him the other day."

Bridgette tilts her head to the side. "We had sex last *night*. How did you tell him before it happened?"

I grin. "I had a good feeling."

She lets her head drop back in defeat, until she's staring up at the ceiling. "I knew it was a bad idea."

"It was a *great* idea," I interject.

She looks at me with as much seriousness as she can muster. "It was a onetime thing, Warren."

I hold up two fingers. "It was twice, actually."

She makes a face that lets me know just how much I'm irritating her. "I'm serious, Warren. We're not doing it again."

"Thank God," I say, slowly stepping toward her. "Because it was awful, wasn't it? I could tell you weren't enjoying it." I continue across the kitchen until I'm less than a foot from touching her. "You especially weren't enjoying the part when you were on your back, and my tongue was . . ."

She slaps her hand over my mouth to shut me up. She's looking at me, narrow-eyed. "I'm serious, Warren. This changes nothing. We aren't a couple. In fact, I'll probably bring other guys home and you need to be prepared for that."

She removes her hand from my mouth and I disagree. "You will not."

She looks at me with a competitive gleam in her eyes. "I will. This is why I warned you not to get clingy."

Ha. She thinks this is clingy? If she smiles and laughs like she did last night, she'll find out just how clingy I can be.

"If you don't want me to want you anymore, it's not that hard," I tell her. "Just don't smile at me." I lean forward until my lips are at her ear. "If you don't smile at me, I won't have the urge to do all those bad things to you. Because your smile is incredible, Bridgette."

I pull away slowly and look down at her. She's attempting to control the rise and fall of her chest, but she's not fooling me. I grin, and the faintest of smiles appears on her lips. I reach my hand up and touch the corner of her mouth with my finger. "You're such a tease."

She pulls away from me and calmly pushes against my chest. She grabs her drink and returns to her bedroom without another word.

I press my head against the cabinet door and sigh heavily. What have I done? What in God's name have I done to myself?

•   •   •

Bridgette and I both had the day off today, and I was positive that after our interaction this morning, and especially after last night, that she'd be all over me by nightfall. However, she completely ignored me. She stayed in her room most of the day, and she wouldn't even acknowledge me. Now it's after eleven at night. I have to be at work tomorrow morning, and I know she has an early class, so my hope for a round three is swiftly dwindling.

She even locked the door when she took a shower earlier.

I sit on the edge of my bed and contemplate the night before, going over every single move in my head, wondering where I went wrong. The only thing I can conclude is that I did nothing wrong. I did everything right, and this scared her, because she's not used to guys taking control over her. I made her feel weak.

She doesn't like to feel weak. She obviously has serious power issues and I messed with her head. This should probably make me feel guilty, but actually I'm proud. I love that I got to her. I love that I'm slowly figuring her out. And the best part is, I have a feeling that she'll be coming back for a repeat. Maybe not tonight, but she'll be back, because she's human. Every human has a weakness and I think I just discovered what hers is.

Me.

I crawl under the covers and close my eyes, but I can already tell I won't be able to sleep. It's as if last night awakened this hunger inside of me and if I don't feed it every night before I go to bed, I'll never fall asleep. I count sheep, I count stars, I repeat Bible verses in my head that I learned when I was five. None of it works, because I'm still here an hour later and I'm still wide awake.

I wonder if *she's* awake.

I wonder if she would open her door if I knocked.

I toss the covers off and begin to walk to my door, but immediately U-turn to the nightstand for a condom. All I have on are boxers, so I slip it beneath the elastic band and open my bedroom door.

Boobs.

Her boobs.

They're right here.

Her hand is in the air, poised to knock on my door. She looks just as shocked that I opened it as I am that she's standing here. She's wearing a black lace bra and the tiniest pair of panties I've ever seen in my life. She lowers her arm and we stare at each other for a solid five seconds before I'm pulling her inside, slamming my door and pushing her up against it. Her tongue is in my mouth faster than I can slip my hand beneath her bra.

"Is this what you sleep in?" I say against her mouth, pulling the straps of her bra down.

"Yes," she says breathlessly. She tilts her head and pushes my face against her neck. "But sometimes I sleep naked."

I groan and press myself against her, ready to sink myself inside her. "I like it." I spin her around until her chest is pressed against the door and her back is to me. I wrap my arm around her and grab one of her breasts while I slide my other hand down to her ass. She's in a thong. A teeny, tiny, black, lacy, beautiful thong. I rub my hand over her and then slip my fingers beneath the thin veil of fabric, pulling it down to her knees. I watch as the thong falls to her ankles and she kicks it aside.

I position myself directly behind her and run my hands down her back and to her waist. "Put your palms against the door."

She doesn't move them right away. I can feel her hesitation. I'm sure she doesn't want to hand over control again, but she needs to realize she lost control the second she showed up at my bedroom door.

I watch as she slowly presses her palms against my bedroom door. I lean forward and brush her hair away from her neck, dropping it over her shoulder. "Thank you," I whisper against her neck. I pull her hips until she's flush against me, and then I remove my boxers and open the condom.

"Bend over a little more," I tell her.

She does. She's such a fast learner.

I wrap my fingers in her hair and twist my hand around until I have a fistful of it, and then I tug just enough to get her to lift her face. She whimpers when I do this, and that little whimper is all it takes for me to push into her, as far as I can go until she's completely full.

"Make that sound again," I whisper.

She doesn't, so I tug at her hair. The noise escapes her throat and it's so beautiful and full of desire. I pull out and push back into her, and the same sound passes her lips. *I can't take it.* I don't know if I can do this standing up, because that sound is making me dizzy.

I cover one of her hands with mine and squeeze, giving myself the wall support I need to continue moving in and out of her. Every time she whimpers, I push into her a little bit harder. She begins to whimper, over and over, occasionally replacing that sound with my name, and *I already know I'm gonna sleep like a rock tonight.*

Right when I feel myself growing close to release, I pull out of her and reposition her so that her back is against the door. I lift her legs and wrap them around my waist, sliding back inside her with ease. I keep one arm wrapped around her waist to hold her up and my other hand pressed against the door for support. My tongue is fighting hers, and I'm swallowing every sound she's willing to give me.

Her hands are gripping my neck, so I reach behind me and pull one of her hands away. I press her palm against her chest and slide it slowly down her stomach. My forehead meets hers, and I look her hard in the eyes. "Touch yourself."

Her eyes grow wide, and she begins to shake her head. I place my hand on top of hers and I look down at where are bodies join together. I move her hand a few more inches until her fingers are right where I want them. "Please," I breathe out, desperately.

I need my hand for support, so I pull it away and press it against the door beside her head. I'm still holding her around the waist with my other arm and slowly pushing in and out of her. Our foreheads are still pressed together, but now my eyes are planted on her hand as she timidly begins to move her fingers in a slow, circular motion.

"Holy shit," I exhale. I watch her for a minute longer, until she starts to relax against her hand, and then I move my eyes back to her face. I pull away and stare down at her, watching as her head falls back against the door. Her eyes are closed and her lips are slightly parted and all I can feel in my heart is *kiss her, kiss her.*

My lips come down gently against hers and she moans softly into my mouth. I tease her lips with the tip of my tongue, sliding it across her top lip and then her bottom. Her moans are becoming more frequent, and the more I press her against the door, the better I can feel her hand moving between us.

I can't believe this is real life. I can't believe she lives five feet away from me and she's willing to give me this part of her. I'm the luckiest man in the world.

She starts to whimper again, but this time my mouth is resting against hers and I take in every single one of the sounds she makes. She tilts her face more and more to mine, wanting me to kiss her hard, but I'm enjoying this too much. I love the way she looks right now, eyes closed, mouth open, heart exposed. I don't want to kiss her. I want to keep my eyes open and watch every second of this.

I stop moving inside her and wait for her to finish, because if I keep moving, I won't last another second. She begins to open her eyes, wondering why I stopped, so I lean in to her ear. "You're almost there," I whisper. "I just want to watch you."

She relaxes again and I continue to watch her, soaking up every whimper and every moan and every movement she makes like I'm a sponge and she's my water.

As soon as her legs begin to tighten around my waist, I grip her hips with both hands and resume moving inside her. Her whimpers turn into moans, and her moans turn into my name and it takes us all of ten seconds before we're both shaking and gasping for breath and kissing and groping and then finally, sighing.

Her body weakens in my arms and she lays her head against my chest. I bring my hand up to her neck and kiss her softly on top of the head.

After a solid minute of working to catch our breath and regain the ability to move, I slowly begin to pull out of her. She lowers her feet to the floor and looks up at me. She's not smiling, but I can see the calmness behind her eyes. This was exactly what she needed. Exactly what *I* needed.

"Thank you," she says, matter-of-factly.

I grin. "You're welcome."

She ducks her head as soon as she begins to smile, and slips under my arm. She enters the bathroom and closes the door behind her. I lean against the wall and slide down to the floor, completely unable to will my legs to make it back to the bed. If I didn't have to wait on her to finish in the bathroom, I'd fall asleep right here on the floor.

Chapter Seven

Three solid weeks.

Twenty-one nights.

Over thirty times we've had sex.

Absolutely zero interaction during the day.

I don't really understand her. I don't know her well enough to know what sets her off or, in turn, what makes her so quiet. I don't know why she refuses to treat what's going on between us like it's anything remotely significant, but I'm not complaining. I mean, come on. We have sex every night and I don't have to dote on her during the day. I would have the perfect setup if I didn't want just a little bit more from her. But until I can get to another level with Bridgette, I know nothing better come in between us. Especially a new roommate, which is what I'm afraid might happen. Brennan has officially gone on tour and moved out, which means his room is now up for grabs. I can't take the idea of Bridgette's sister moving in, which is something I've heard them discussing on the phone. I don't know what or whom Ridge has in mind, but I for sure don't think I can take the possibility of another guy moving in. As much as I want to pretend I'm as casual with this arrangement as Bridgette is, if another guy even looks at her ass in those shorts, I won't be able to refrain from beating his ass. And I'm not even the type of guy who fights other guys, but Bridgette makes me want to fight everyone. Even the nerdy guys. I'll hit all the humans if it means keeping up the arrangement I've got going with her.

Which is why I can't stop staring at the couch right now. There's a person on it. I think it's a girl, because I see blond hair peeking out from under the pillow pulled over her face, but it could be a long-haired guy. A guy I don't want to be our next roommate. I continue to watch the couch, waiting for the person to wake up. I'm loud enough in the kitchen to wake up the whole apartment, but whoever is on this couch is sleeping like a rock.

I finish pouring my bowl of cereal and bring it into the living room. Since whoever this is has decided to take up residence where I eat breakfast, I take a seat on the floor, right in front of the couch. I begin eating, crunching as loud as I can.

I wonder if she or he is a friend of Bridgette's.

No, Bridgette didn't bring anyone home last night. I know this because I picked her up after I got off work and we came straight home and went straight to my bed. Come to think of it, we didn't even turn on the living room lights, so I'm pretty sure whoever this is was probably on the couch last night, we just didn't notice.

Oh, man. I wonder if we were loud? We never have to worry about how loud we are when Ridge is home.

A groan comes from beneath the pillow and the body rolls over, facing me so I can see it is, in fact, a girl. I continue to sit on the floor, eating my cereal. I watch her attempt to open her eyes.

"Who are you and why are you asleep on my couch?" I finally ask her.

Her whole body jerks at the sound of my voice. She lifts the pillow and backs away, making eye contact with me. I have to stifle a laugh, because someone has written *Someone wrote on your forehead* on her face with a Sharpie.

It was more than likely Ridge, so I do what I can to avoid looking at it and stare at her eyes instead.

"Are you the new roommate?" I say with a mouthful of cereal.

She shakes her head. "No," she says. "I'm a friend of Ridge's."

Hmmm. Didn't see that one coming.

"Ridge only has one friend. Me."

She rolls her eyes and sits up on the couch. She's cute. *Very impressive, Ridge.*

"Jealous?" she asks, stretching into a yawn.

"What's his last name?"

"Whose last name?"

"Your very good friend, Ridge."

She sighs and her head falls against the back of the couch. "I don't know Ridge's last name," she says. "I don't even know his middle name. The only thing I know about him is he's got a mean right hook. And I'm only asleep on your couch because my boyfriend of two years decided it would be fun to screw my roommate and I really didn't want to stick around to watch."

I like this girl. She could give Bridgette a run for her money. And I don't mean with *me*, I just mean because Bridgette is mean and probably doesn't meet a lot of girls who would stand up to her. This could be fun. "It's Lawson," I say. "And he doesn't have a middle name."

I hear Bridgette's bedroom door open and I immediately turn around to face her. She's still wearing my boxer shorts from last night, but she's put her own T-shirt over them. *God, she looks good.* "Good morning, Bridgette. Sleep well?"

She looks at me briefly and rolls her eyes. "Screw you, Warren."

Which, in Bridgette speak means, *Yes, Warren. I slept like a baby, thanks to you.*

"That's Bridgette," I whisper, turning back to the girl on the couch. "She pretends to hate me during the day, but at night she *loves* me."

The girl laughs and makes a face like she doesn't believe me.

"Shit!" Bridgette yells. I turn around in time to watch her catch herself by grabbing the bar. "Jesus Christ!" She kicks one of the suitcases that are still on the floor next to the bar. "Tell your little friend if she's staying here she needs to take her shit to her room!"

My little friend? I turn to face the girl on the couch again, wide-eyed. I think Bridgette already has an issue with this girl. All the more reason to make sure she becomes the new roommate, because I like an angry Bridgette. I'm also willing to bet a jealous Bridgette will be a lot more clingy, which could work in my favor. I turn and glare at Bridgette from where I'm seated. "What am I, your bitch? Tell her yourself."

Bridgette glances at the girl on the couch, then points to the suitcase she almost tripped over. "GET . . . YOUR . . . SHIT . . . OUT . . . OF . . . THE . . . KITCHEN!" she says before marching back to her bedroom.

I slowly turn my head to face the girl again. "Why does she think you're deaf?"

She shrugs. "I have no idea. She came to that conclusion last night and I failed to correct her."

I laugh. What a perfect prank, and I didn't even have to think of it. "Oh, this is classic," I say to her. "Do you have any pets?"

She shakes her head.

"Are you opposed to porn?"

"Not opposed to the principle of porn, but slightly opposed to being *featured* in one." I nod, because that's probably a good thing. At least I won't have double the reason to watch every porn I can get my hands on.

"Do you have annoying friends?"

"My best friend is a backstabbing whore and I'm no longer speaking to her."

"What are your showering habits?"

She laughs. "Once a day, with a skipped day every now and then. No more than fifteen minutes."

"Do you cook?"

"Only when I'm hungry."

"Do you clean up after yourself?"

"Probably better than you," she says, glancing at my shirt, which I've used for a napkin several times during this conversation.

"Do you listen to disco?"

"I'd rather eat barbed wire."

She's perfect for us.

"All right, then," I tell her. "I guess you can stay."

She sits up straighter and pulls her legs onto the couch. "I didn't realize I was being interviewed."

I look at her suitcase and then back at her. Most people don't travel with all their belongings, and if she's in search of somewhere to live, I want it to be here so I can ensure the new roommate doesn't have a dick. "It's obvious you need a place to stay, and we've got an empty room. If you don't take it, Bridgette wants to move her sister in next month and that's the *last* thing Ridge and I need."

"I can't stay here," she says, shaking her head.

"Why not? From the sound of it, you're about to spend the day searching for an apartment anyway. What's wrong with this one? You won't even have to walk very far to get here."

The door to Ridge's bedroom opens and I can see the girl's eyes widen slightly, as if she's nervous. That's probably not a good sign for Ridge, but he's so hung up on Maggie, adding this chick as a roommate shouldn't be an issue for any of us. I wink at her and stand up to walk my bowl back to the kitchen. I speak and sign at the same time. "Have you met our new roommate?"

Ridge glances at her and then looks back at me. "Yeah," he signs. "She needs a place to stay, so I'll probably just let her use Brennan's room. Or if you want, she can take your room and you can take Brennan's, so we both aren't having to share a bathroom with girls."

I shake my head. "No way are you putting me further away from Bridgette. Our bathroom sex is my favorite."

Ridge shakes his head. "You're pathetic." He walks back to his room and I look at our new roommate.

"What did he say?" she asks, nervously.

"Exactly what I thought he'd say," I tell her. I walk to my room and grab my keys off the dresser. I glance into the bathroom and see Bridgette at the sink. I swing the door open and give her a quick kiss on the cheek. She tries to pull away from me, but I also see the smile tugging at her lips.

My eyes fall to the black Sharpie sitting next to the sink. I pick it up and eye Bridgette suspiciously. She shrugs her shoulders and I laugh.

I didn't think she had it in her, but after the water cup prank and now this, I fear I might have met my match. At least the new roommate is being hazed early.

I close the bathroom door and head back out into the living room. "He says you two already worked out a deal." I point to Brennan's old room. "Heading to work now. That's your room if you want to put your stuff in it. You might have to throw all Brennan's shit in the corner, though." I open the door and step outside, but turn around before I close it. "Oh. What's your name?"

"Sydney."

"Well, Sydney. Welcome to the weirdest place you'll ever live."

I close the door behind me, feeling slightly guilty that I may have swayed this roommate thing a little in my favor. But seriously. Not only does this ensure our new roommate won't be putting the moves on Bridgette, it also makes for an interesting dynamic. Two girls in a prank war may be the best thing that ever happened to Ridge and me.

Chapter Eight

"So, what's with the new roommate?" I sign to Ridge when I walk in the door.

"She lives in the complex. Her boyfriend cheated on her and she needed a place to stay."

I walk over to the table he's seated at and pull the chair out. "She still here?"

He looks up from the laptop and nods. "Yeah, she'll probably be here for a few weeks, at least. That okay?"

Something is off with him. When you've known someone most of your life, you can almost feel their unease. This Sydney girl makes him nervous, and I don't know why.

"Is Maggie okay with it?"

His attention quickly moves back to his laptop. He nods his head and stops signing. I push my chair out and glance at the door to see if Bridgette's shoes are where she always keeps them. They aren't. I tap Ridge on the shoulder. "Where's Bridgette?" I sign.

He shifts in his seat. "Out."

"Out where?"

He shrugs. "Warren, do you really want to know? Because you aren't going to like it."

I sit in the chair again. "Hell yes, I want to know. Where is she?"

He leans back in his chair and sighs. "A guy picked her up about three hours ago. It looked like they were going out."

"Out," I sign. "Out like on a date?"

He nods.

I suddenly want to punch Ridge, but I know he has nothing to do with it. I stand up and push the chair back under the table.

She's on a date. Bridgette is on a fucking date.

This is such bullshit. Why didn't I set boundaries? Why didn't I tell her she couldn't see other guys?

What if she brings him back here? She will. She's so mean, she probably will.

I grab my keys and sign to Ridge that I'll be back in a little while.

I'll fix this.

Somehow.

• • •

I'm seated on the couch two hours later when the door opens. As expected, she doesn't walk in alone. A guy is following behind her, way too close. His hand is on her lower back as she slips her shoes off at the door and looks straight at me. "Oh. Hey, Warren."

She points to me. "Guy, this is Warren. Warren, this is Guy."

I look at him. At all six-metrosexual-douchebag-feet of him. "Your name is *Guy*?"

He doesn't respond. He just looks at Bridgette like he's a little uncomfortable that he just walked into her apartment and a guy is sitting on her couch. I bet he'd be really uncomfortable to know what I was doing on this same couch with Bridgette just twenty-four hours ago.

"Warren," Bridgette says in a sickeningly fake, sweet voice. "Do you mind giving us some privacy?" She glances toward my bedroom, silently asking if I'll go wait it out in there while she flirts in my living room with *Guy*. I narrow my eyes at her. She's doing this on purpose. She's testing me, and I'm about to ace this test.

"Sure will, Bridgette," I say with a smile. I stand up and walk over to Guy, reaching out for his hand. "Good to meet you," I say to him. He smiles and his apprehension eases when he sees I've loosened up. "You kiddos have fun. I'll leave the bathroom door unlocked in case either of you needs to use it." I point toward the bathroom, planting the seed.

Please, let him have to use the restroom. Please.

Bridgette can see that my last comment was out of character. She squints her eyes at me as I retreat to my room. I close the door and stay right next to it. I'm not about to miss a second of this. If she's going to try and test me or torture me by bringing another guy home, she has to expect I'll eavesdrop on their entire conversation.

I stand with my ear pressed to the door for at least fifteen minutes. In those fifteen minutes, I hear him go on and on about everything he's good at.

Baseball.

Football.

Tennis.

Trivia. (He actually forced her to quiz him.)

Work. (He's a salesman. He's the best, apparently. Highest sales for the last four quarters.)

He's a world traveler, *of course*.

He speaks French, *of course*.

Bridgette yawns four times during their conversation. I feel like this act she's putting on is exhausting her more than it is me.

"Mind if I use your restroom?" Guy says.

Finally.

A few seconds later, I hear the door close to the restroom and I immediately open my bedroom door and walk to the kitchen. Bridgette is seated on the couch with her feet propped up on the coffee table. "You look bored to death," I tell her.

"He's riveting," she says with a fake smile. "I'm having so much fun, I'll probably ask him to stay the night."

I smile, knowing that won't happen. "He'll never agree to that, Bridgette," I tell her. "In fact"—I look down at my wrist and tap it—"I'm pretty sure he'll be leaving as soon as he exits the restroom."

She sits up straight on the couch and then comes to a quick stand. She stalks over to me, pointing her finger, pushing it against my chest. "What did you do, Warren?"

The bathroom door opens and Guy walks out. Bridgette faces him with her obnoxious, fake smile. "Want to hang out in my room?" she says, walking toward him.

He glances at me and I shake my head, quickly. For all he knows, I'm just warning him, man-to-man, that he better run while he still can.

I can tell he's terrified after seeing what all I've planted in the restroom. He glances at the door and back at Bridgette. "Actually, I was just about to leave," he says. "I'll call you."

The next few seconds are the most awkward seconds I've ever seen play out between two people. He reaches in for a handshake, she goes in for a hug, he backs away, afraid she's about to try to kiss him, and his eyes grow wide with fear. He rushes around her and heads straight for the door. "Nice to meet you, Warren. I'll call you later, Bridgette."

And he's gone.

She slowly turns to face me. Her eyes are as sharp as diamonds. I'm scared they're sharp enough to slit my throat. I wipe the smile from my face and walk toward my bedroom. "Good night, Bridgette."

Nice try, Bridgette.

Nice try.

       •   •   •

"Son of a bitch!"

My bathroom door swings open and she marches straight toward my bed. I was studying, but I quickly throw my books aside when I see her coming at me. She jumps onto the bed, standing, and walks across it. She holds her hands up in the air and that's when I notice she's holding something. I notice it too late, though, because the cream squirts out of the tube and onto the top of my head.

"*Hemorrhoid* cream?" she yells, tossing it aside. She grabs another tube of cream that was tucked under her arm.

"*Wart* remover?" She squeezes it onto my pillow. I'm trying to cover my head with the blanket, but she's getting the stuff everywhere. I pull her legs out from under her and she falls on the bed, then she starts kicking me, and throwing the tubes at me.

"*Cold sore relief?*" She squirts that one right in my face. "I can't believe you put all these in our bathroom! I swear to God, you're a little boy, Warren. A jealous little boy!"

I pull the rest of the tubes from her hands and I wrestle her onto her back, locking her arms to the mattress.

"You're such an *asshole*," she yells.

I struggle to hold her still. "If I'm an asshole, then you're a coldhearted, calculating, ruthless *bitch!*"

She grunts, trying to free herself from my grip. I refuse to budge, but I also do my best to remove the anger from my voice and speak to her calmly.

"What was that about, Bridgette? Huh? Why the hell did you bring him here?"

She stops struggling long enough to smile in my face. Knowing that my jealousy makes her smile pisses me off even more. I hold both of her wrists with one hand and reach beside her head, grabbing a tube of the cream. I flip the lid open and squirt it in her hair. She starts thrashing beneath me and *God, I'm so mad at her.*

Why would she do that?

I grab her jaw and hold her face so she'll look at me. She realizes she's not overpowering me physically, so she relents. Her chest is heaving and she's gasping for breath. I can see anger in her eyes. I have no idea what gives her the right to be mad, when she's the one fucking with my head.

I lower my forehead to hers and close my eyes. "Why?" I say, breathless. The room grows quiet. "Why did you bring him here?"

She sighs and turns her head. I pull back and look down on her, convinced I see more pain in her features than anger. Her voice is quiet when she speaks. "Why'd you let another girl move in today?"

I know that was hard for her, because her question proves that she cares. That question proves that I wasn't the only one fearing a new roommate would come between us. She's scared I'll move on. She's scared that Sydney is going to come between us, so she tried to hurt me first.

"You think things might change between us just because another girl moved in?" I ask her. She looks over my shoulder so she doesn't have to look me in the eyes. I tilt her jaw and make her look at me. "Is that why you brought him here?"

Her eyes narrow and she tightens her lips, refusing to admit she was hurt.

"Just say it," I beg. I need her to say it out loud. All I need is for her to admit she brought him here because she was hurt and scared. I need her to admit that there's an actual heart inside her chest. And that sometimes it beats for me.

Since she won't admit it, I'll admit it *for* her. "You've never let anyone close enough to where their absence could hurt you. But it would hurt you if I left you, so you wanted to hurt me first." I press my lips closer to her ear. "You did," I whisper. "Seeing you walk through that door with him hurt like hell. But I'm not going anywhere, Bridgette, and I'm not interested in anyone else. So that little game you tried to play backfired, because from now on, the only man you're allowed to bring home is the one who already lives here." I slowly pull back and look her in the eyes. "Understood?"

In true Bridgette form, she refuses to answer. But I also

know that her refusal to answer is her way of saying I'm right and that she agrees.

She's breathing so much heavier than she was a few minutes ago. I'm almost certain I am, too, because it doesn't feel like my lungs are working anymore. I can't inhale, no matter how hard I try, because the need to kiss her has taken over my passageways. *I need her air.*

I force my mouth against hers and I kiss her with a possessiveness I didn't even know was in me. I kiss her so desperately, I forget that I'm still mad at her. My tongue dives into her mouth and she takes it, giving me her own desperate kiss in return, grabbing at my face, pulling me closer. I can feel her in this kiss like I've never felt her before. It's probably the best kiss I've ever experienced with her, because it's the first kiss with actual emotions behind it.

Even though it's the best kiss, it's also one of the shortest. She shoves me away from her. She's out of my bed, out of my bedroom, and out of my line of sight as the bathroom door slams behind her. I roll onto my back and stare up at the ceiling.

She's so confusing. She's so frustrating. She's so damn unpredictable.

She's nothing I've ever wanted in a girl. And absolutely everything I need.

I hear the water in the shower start running, so I immediately roll off the bed and walk into the bathroom. My heart tightens a little when the doorknob turns and I realize she didn't lock it behind her. I know this sign means she wants me to follow her. What she wants me to do once I'm inside this bathroom is a mystery, though. Does she want me to take her against the shower wall? Does she want me to apologize to her? Does she want me to talk to her?

I don't know with her. I never know. So, I do what I always do and wait for her to show me what she needs. I walk into the bathroom and grab a towel to wipe all the damn cream out of my hair. I get as much out as I can and then close the lid to the toilet and take a seat on it, listening quietly as she continues her shower. I know she knows I'm in here, but she doesn't speak. I'd even take her insults right now if it meant she would say something to alleviate the silence.

I lean forward and clasp my hands between my knees. "Does this scare you, Bridgette?"

I know she hears me, but she doesn't answer. *That means yes.*

I let my head fall into my hands and I vow to remain calm. This is how she relates. She doesn't know any different. Somehow, over the course of her twenty-two years, she's never learned how to love, or even communicate, really. That's not her fault.

"Have you ever been in love before?"

It's a slightly generic question. I don't ask if she could fall in love with me *specifically*, so maybe the question won't piss her off.

I hear a relenting sigh come from behind the shower curtain. "I think it takes *being* loved in order to know *how* to love," she says quietly. "So I guess that's a no."

I wince at her answer. What a sad, sad answer. One I wasn't expecting.

"You can't really believe that, Bridgette."

Silence follows. She doesn't reply.

"Your mother loved you," I say to her.

"My mother gave me to my grandmother when I was six months old."

"I'm sure your grandmother loved you."

A quiet, pained laugh comes from the shower. "I'm sure she did, but not enough to stay alive for more than a year. After she died I lived with my aunt, who made it very obvious that she didn't love me. My *uncle* did, though. Just in all the wrong ways."

I squeeze my eyes shut and allow her words to sink in. Brennan wasn't kidding when he said she's had a rough life. And she's so casual about it, like she's just accepted that this is the kind of life she was given and there's nothing she can do about it. A mixture of anger and sadness consumes me.

"Bridgette . . ."

"Don't bother, Warren. I've dealt with my life the only way I know how. It works for me, and I don't need you or anyone else to try and figure me out, or fix me. I am who I am and I've accepted that."

I clamp my mouth shut and don't offer her words of advice. I wouldn't know what to say anyway. I feel awful for wanting to prod her with more questions after that revelation, but I'm not sure when I'll get this side of her again. Bridgette doesn't open up easily, and now I can see why. She doesn't seem to have had anyone to open up to, so this might be a first for her.

"What about your sister?"

Bridgette releases a sigh. "She's not even my real sister. We're stepsisters, and we didn't even grow up in the same house."

I should stop with the questions. I know I should, but I can't. To know that she's probably never spoken or heard the words "I love you" from anyone in her life is affecting me way more than I imagined it could.

"I'm sure you've had boyfriends who have loved you in the past."

She laughs a really sad laugh, and then she just sighs an even sadder sigh. "If you're planning on asking me questions like this all night, I'd much rather you just fuck me."

I cover my mouth with my hand, absorbing her words like a knife to the chest. She seriously can't be this broken. No one can be this alone, can they?

"Have you ever loved *anyone*, Bridgette?"

Silence. Complete silence until her voice shatters it like glass. "It's hard to fall in love with assholes, Warren."

That's a comment from a girl who's been jaded way too many times. I stand up and slide the shower curtain open. She's standing beneath the stream of water. Mascara has streaked its way down her cheeks.

"Maybe you just haven't met the right asshole yet."

She immediately lets out a quick burst of laughter, along with a few tears. Her eyes are sad, and her smile is appreciative, and for the first time she's completely bare. It's as though she's holding her heart out to me, begging me not to break it. The vulnerability she's showing me right now is something I'm almost positive she's never shown anyone else. No other man, at least.

I step into the shower. She looks at me in shock as my clothes quickly become drenched. I take her face in my hands, and I kiss her.

I don't kiss her fast.

I don't kiss her rough.

I don't kiss her hard.

I press my lips to hers with such delicacy; I want her to feel everything she's ever deserved to feel at the hands of someone else. She deserves to feel beautiful. She deserves to feel important. She deserves to feel cared for. She deserves to feel respected. She deserves to feel like there's at least one other person in this world who accepts her for exactly who she is.

She deserves to know how *I* feel, because I feel all of those things. And maybe a little more.

Chapter Nine

Since that day in the shower, things have changed between us.

Not that she had this miraculous personality shift or that she's actually nice to me during the day. In fact, she's still pretty damn mean to me most of the time. She also still thinks Sydney is deaf, which is almost unbelievable that the prank has gone on for this long. So I can't even say that my excitement over pranking her has changed.

What *has* changed are our nights together.

The sex.

It's different now. Slower. Way more eye contact. Way more kissing. Way more buildup. Way more kissing. So much kissing, and not just on the mouth. She kisses me everywhere, and she takes her time when she does it. And she enjoys it.

She still isn't the type to want to cuddle afterward, and she always kicks me out of her bed before the sun comes up.

But still, it's different. That night in the shower tore a wall down between us. Because I know that every night when I have her in bed, she gives me a part of herself that no one else has ever seen. And that's enough to keep me happy for a long damn time.

I just hope today doesn't ruin that.

We both have the day off and that doesn't happen very often between both of our jobs and school. I have a few errands to run and I asked her to go with me, which might be a little strange. We've been sleeping together for a few months now, but this is the first time we've ever actually done anything that didn't involve sex.

Which also makes me wonder if I should ask her out on a date eventually. I know she's not a typical girl, but surely she likes some of the same things other girls do, like being taken out on dates. But she's never hinted that she wants me to take her on one, and frankly, I'm scared to ask her. I feel like our setup is perfect for both of us and if we start throwing dates into the mix, it'll screw it all up.

That includes daytime dates. Like today. Like what we're about to do.

Shit.

"So," Sydney says. She's seated on the couch next to me. I'm watching porn, naturally, because Bridgette still refuses to give me the name of the one she was in. Sydney doesn't mind it, though. She's focusing on her homework, oblivious to the fact that I'm kind of having a minor internal freak-out over the fact that I may or may not have just invited Bridgette on a daytime date to run errands.

"What's up with Bridgette?"

I glance at Sydney and she's still focusing on her textbook, making notes.

"What do you mean?"

Sydney shrugs. "She's just so . . . mean."

I laugh, because it's true. Bridgette can be awful. "She can't help it," I say. "She's had a rough life."

"So has Ridge," Sydney says, "but he doesn't bite people's heads off when they try to speak to him."

"That's because Ridge is deaf. He can't yell at people, it's physically impossible for him."

Sydney looks up at me and rolls her eyes, laughing. She elbows me in the ribs, just as Bridgette walks out of her bedroom. Bridgette glares at Sydney and I hate that she still assumes there could ever be something between Sydney and me. I like her, and I think she's cool, but I have a feeling Ridge would put a stop to that in a heartbeat.

Which isn't a good thing, considering Ridge has Maggie. But those are issues I don't feel like getting involved in at the moment, because *my* issue is glaring right at me. "Please don't tell me you invited your little girlfriend," Bridgette says, shifting her eyes toward Sydney.

Sydney is really good at this prank thing. She doesn't even bat an eye as Bridgette talks about her. She just goes on pretending she can't hear a word Bridgette says. I'm pretty sure Sydney has gone on this long with the prank because it's a whole lot easier than having to actually *speak* to Bridgette.

"She's not coming," I say, standing up. "She has plans."

Bridgette turns away, giving her attention to the purse she has just slung over her shoulder. I walk up to her and wrap my arms around her from behind. "I'm kidding," I whisper in her ear. "I didn't invite anyone else to run errands with me today but you."

Bridgette's hand meets my forehead, and she pushes me away from her. "I'll stay here if you expect today to be like this."

I take a step back. "Like what?"

She points at me. "You. Touching me. Kissing me. PDA.

Gross." She walks to the front door and I clutch my hand to my heart and wince at Sydney.

"Good luck," she mouths as I make my way to the door.

Once we're in my car and it's moving away from the apartment, Bridgette finally speaks. "So where are we going first? I need to go to Walgreens before we come back."

"First, we go to my sister's house, then we go to the bank, then we go to Walgreens, then we go eat lunch, then we go home."

Her hand flies up and she holds up a finger. "What did you just say?"

I repeat myself. "First we go to my sister's house, then we go to . . ."

"Why in the *hell* are you taking me to your sister's house? I don't want to meet your sister, Warren. We aren't that kind of couple."

I roll my eyes and grab the hand she's holding up in protest. "I'm not bringing you as my girlfriend. You can stay in the damn car for all I care. I just need to drop off a package at her house."

This actually eases her apprehension. She relaxes into the seat and flips her hand over so that I can slide my fingers through hers. I look down at our hands and seeing them linked together on the seat between us feels like I just went further with her than the night we first had sex.

She would have never let me hold her hand back then. Hell, she would have never let me hold her hand last month. But we're holding hands now.

Maybe I should ask her out on a date.

She pulls her hand from mine and I immediately glance

up at her. She's staring straight at me. "You were smiling too much," she says.

What?

I reach over and grab her hand again and pull it back to me. "I was smiling because I like holding your hand."

She yanks her hand back. "I know. That's why I don't want you to hold it."

Goddammit. She's not winning this one.

I reach across the seat again, swerving the car in the process. She tries to shove her hand beneath her legs so that I can't grasp it, so I pull at her wrist instead. I release the steering wheel and reach across with both hands now, steering with my knee. "Give me your hand," I say through clenched teeth. "I want to hold your damn hand." I have to grab the wheel to steer us back into our lane. Once we're no longer in danger of crashing, I slam on the brakes as I pull over to the side of the road. I throw the car in park and lock the doors so she can't run. I know how she works.

I lean across the seat and pry her hand away from being tucked against her chest. I grab her wrist with both hands and I pull her toward me. She's still trying to fight me by pulling her hand away, so I release her and look her directly in the eye. "Give. Me. Your. Hand."

I'm not sure if I just scared her a little, but she relaxes and allows me to grab her wrist. I put her wrist in my left hand and I hold up my right hand in front of hers. "Spread your fingers."

She makes a fist instead.

I pry open her fist, then force our fingers to intertwine. I hate that she's being so resistant. She's pissing me the hell off. All I want to do is hold her damn hand and she's making such a big deal out of it. We're doing everything backward in this relationship. Couples are supposed to start out holding hands and going on dates. Not us. We start out fighting, end up screwing, yet we apparently haven't even made it to the point where we can hold hands. If things continue at this rate, we'll probably move in together before we even go on our first date.

I squeeze her hand until I know she can't pull away from me. I scoot back to my seat and I put the car in drive with my left hand and then ease back onto the road.

We drive the next several miles in silence, and she occasionally tries to ease her hand from mine, but each time she does it I squeeze a little tighter and get even more agitated with her. She's gonna hold my damn hand whether she likes it or not.

We hit a red light and the lack of movement outside the car and the lack of conversation inside the car shifts the mood tremendously, thickening the air with tension and . . . *laughter?*

She's laughing at me.

Figures.

I slowly tilt my head in her direction, giving her a side-long glance. She's covering her mouth with her free hand, trying not to laugh, but she is. She's laughing so hard that her body is shaking.

I have no idea what she finds so funny, but I'm not laughing with her. And as much as I want to turn away and punch the steering wheel, I can't stop watching her. I watch the tears form at the corners of her eyes, and I watch her chest heave when she attempts to catch her breath. I watch her lick her lips as she tries to stop herself from smiling so much. I watch her run her free hand through her hair as she sighs, coming down from her fit of laughter.

She finally looks at me. She's no longer laughing, but the residue is still there. The smile is still on her mouth and her cheeks are still a shade pinker than normal, and her mascara is smudged at the corners of her eyes. She shakes her head, keeping her focus on me. "You're insane, Warren." She laughs again, but only for a second. The fact that I'm not smiling is making her uncomfortable.

"Why am I insane?"

"Because," she says. "Who throws that big a fit over holding someone's hand?"

I don't move a muscle. "*You* do, Bridgette."

The smile slowly leaves her face, because she knows I'm right. She knows that she's the one who made a big deal out of holding hands. It was me who wanted to show her how easy it was.

We both look down at our hands as I slowly pry my fingers away from hers and release my grip. The light turns green as I grab the steering wheel and press on the gas. "You sure do know how to make a guy feel like shit, Bridgette."

I give my full attention back to the road and rest my left elbow on the window. I cover my mouth with my hand, squeezing the stress out of my jaw.

We make it three blocks.

Three blocks is all it takes for her to do the most considerate thing she's ever done for me since the moment I met her.

She reaches to the steering wheel and takes my hand.

She pulls it to her lap and slides her fingers between mine. She doesn't stop there, though. Her right hand slides over the top of my hand and she strokes it. She strokes my fingers and the top of my hand and my wrist and back down to my fingers. She stares out her window the whole time, but I can feel her. I can feel her speaking to me and holding me and making love to me, all in the motion of her hands.

And I smile the entire way to my sister's house.

· · ·

"Is she older or younger than you?" Bridgette asks when I turn off the ignition.

"Ten years older."

We both exit the car and begin walking toward the house. I didn't ask her to come with me, but the fact that she didn't wait in the car is proof that another wall has been torn down between us.

I walk up the steps, but before I knock on the door, I turn and face her. "What do you want me to introduce you as?" I ask her. "Roommate? Friend? Girlfriend?"

She glances away and shrugs. "I don't care, really. Just don't make it weird."

I smile and knock on the door. I immediately hear tiny footsteps and squealing and things falling and *shit, I forget how crazy it is over here.* I probably should have warned her.

The door swings open and my nephew, Brody, jumps up and down. "Uncle Warren!" he yells, clapping his hands. I open the screen door, set the package my mother sent for my sister on the floor and immediately swoop Brody up. "Where's your mom?"

He points across the living room. "In the kitchen," he says. His hand meets my cheek and he makes me face him. "Wanna play dead?"

I nod and set him down on the carpet. I motion for Bridgette to follow me inside, and then I fake stab Brody in the chest. He falls to the floor in a dramatic display of defeat.

Bridgette and I both stand over him as he writhes in pain. His body convulses a few times and then his head falls limp to the carpet.

"He dies better than any four-year-old I've ever seen," I say to Bridgette.

She nods, still staring down at him. "I'm in awe," she says.

"Brody!" my sister yells from the kitchen. "Is that Warren?"

I begin walking in the direction of the kitchen and Bridgette follows me. When I round the corner, Whitney has Conner on her hip and she's stirring something on the stove with her other arm.

"Brody's dead, but yeah, it's me," I say to her.

As soon as Whitney glances at me, cries come from the baby monitor next to the stove. She sighs, exasperated, and motions for me to come to the stove. I walk over to her and take the spoon from her hands. "It has to be stirred for at least another minute, then remove the burner from the pan."

"You mean remove the pan from the burner?"

"Whatever," she says. She pulls Conner off her hip and walks toward Bridgette. "Here, hold Conner. I'll be right back."

Bridgette instinctively holds out her hands and my sister

shoves Conner at her. Bridgette's arms are outstretched, as far from her body as she can get them. She's holding Conner under his armpits, staring at me wide-eyed.

"What do I do with it?" she whispers. Her eyes are filled with terror.

"Have you never held a kid before?" I ask in disbelief. Bridgette immediately shakes her head.

"I don't know any kids."

"Me a kid," Conner says.

Bridgette gasps and looks at Conner, who is staring right back at her with just as much terror and fascination. "It talked!" she exclaims. "Oh, my God, you talked!"

Conner grins.

"Say *cat*," Bridgette says.

"Cat," Conner repeats.

She laughs nervously, but is still holding him like he's a dirty towel. I remove the pot from the burner and turn it off, then walk over to her. "Conner's the easy one," I tell her. "Here, hold him like this." I pull him around to her hip and wrap her arm behind him, securing him against her waist. She's trading nervous glances between Conner and me.

"He won't shit on me, will he?"

I laugh and Conner giggles. He slaps her chest twice and kicks his legs. "Shit on me," he says, still laughing.

Bridgette's hand clamps over her mouth. "Oh, my God, he's just like a parrot," she says.

"Warren!" Whitney yells from the top of the stairs.

"I'll be right back."

Bridgette shakes her head and points to Conner. "But . . . but . . . *this* . . ." she stutters.

I pat her on top of her head. "You'll be fine. Just keep him alive for two minutes." I scale the steps and Whitney is standing in the doorway to the nursery. She's wiping her neck with a rag.

"He pissed in my face," she says. She looks so frazzled. I want to hug her, and I would if she weren't covered in infant piss. She hands me the baby. "Take him downstairs while I jump in the shower, please."

I lift him out of her hands. "No problem."

She begins to head to her room, but pauses right before I make it back to the stairs. "Hey," she says. I turn and face her. "Who's the girl?" she signs.

I love that she signs this, so Bridgette has no chance of hearing her ask. Having a family that is all fluent in sign language definitely comes in handy.

"Just my roommate," I sign back to her, shrugging it off. She smiles and walks into her room. I walk down the stairs holding the baby against my chest. I step over Brody, who is still playing dead on the floor. When I make it to the doorway in the kitchen, I pause. Bridgette has sat Conner on the kitchen island. She's standing right in front of him so that he doesn't fall and she's holding up her fingers, counting with him.

"Three. Can you count to three?"

Conner touches his finger to the tips of hers. "One. Two. Twee," he says. They both start clapping and he says, "Me now."

Bridgette begins to count his fingers this time. I lean my head against the doorframe and watch her interact with him.

I don't know why I've never spent time with her outside

of the bedroom before this. I could add up all the things she's done to me at night, and I'm positive I wouldn't trade today for all of that combined.

This is the Bridgette that *I* see. The part of her she gives to me. And now that I'm watching her, I see that she's very capable of giving it to others who deserve it.

"Do you stare at all your roommates like this?" Whitney whispers in my ear. I spin around, and she's standing behind me, watching me watch Bridgette. I shake my head and look back at Bridgette. "No. I don't."

As soon as I say it, I regret saying it. Whitney will be texting me within the hour, wanting to know all the details. How long I've known her, where she's from, if I'm in love with her.

Time to leave.

"Ready, Bridgette?" I ask, handing the baby back to Whitney.

Bridgette glances up at me and then back to Conner. She actually looks a little sad that she has to say goodbye.

"Bye, Bwidjet," Conner says to her with a wave. Bridgette gasps and turns to face me.

"Oh, my God! Warren, he said my name!"

She turns back to Conner, and he's still waving. "Shit on me," he says.

Bridgette immediately picks him up and sets him down on the floor. "Ready," she says quickly, walking away from him and toward the front door.

Whitney is pointing at Conner and looking at me, "Did he just say . . ."

I nod. "I think he did, Whit. You need to watch your

language around your kids." I give her a quick kiss on the cheek and head for the front door.

Bridgette is standing over Brody, looking down at him. "Seriously impressive."

He's in the exact same position we left him in. "I told you he dies better than anyone I know." I step over him and hold the front door open for her. We walk outside and she doesn't even flinch or pull away when I slide my hand through hers. I walk her to the passenger side door, but before I open it, I turn her to face me and I press her against the car. My hand touches her forehead and I wipe away a wisp of hair.

"I never thought I wanted kids," she says, glancing back at the house.

"But you do now?"

She shakes her head. "No, not really. But maybe if I could have Conner. At that age, for like a year, maybe two. Then I'd probably get tired of him and not want him anymore, but a year or two out of my life might be fun."

I laugh. "So why don't you kidnap him and bring him back when he's five?"

She faces me again. "But you would know it was me who took him."

I smile down at her. "I would never tell. I like you better than I like him."

She shakes her head. "You love your sister too much to do that to her. It would never work. We'd have to kidnap someone else's kid."

I sigh. "Yeah, you're probably right. Besides, we should probably kidnap a celebrity's kid. That way we could get ransom out of it and never have to work again. We could give the kid back, take the money, and spend the rest of our lives having sex all day."

Bridgette smiles. "You're so romantic, Warren. No other guy has ever promised me a kidnapping and ransom."

I tilt her chin up so that her mouth is positioned closer to mine. "Like I said, you just haven't met the right asshole." I press my lips to hers and kiss her, briefly. I keep it PG in case Brody has come back to life and is watching us.

I reach behind her and open the door. She walks around me to climb inside, but before she does, she stands on her tiptoes and kisses me on the cheek.

To Brody or anyone else watching, that was just a kiss on the cheek. But knowing Bridgette like I know her, that was a whole lot more than just a kiss. That was her saying she doesn't need anyone else.

That kiss on the cheek means we're official.

That kiss on the cheek means I have a girlfriend.

Chapter Ten

"So you think it's official because she kissed you on the cheek?" Sydney says, confused. She doesn't get it. She's like everyone else and sees Bridgette at face value, which is fine. Bridgette gives people a pretty rough face value, and that's Bridgette's right.

I stop trying to explain to Sydney my relationship with Bridgette. Besides, I kind of like that no one gets it. And even though we had this really crazy, nonsexual experience with the hand-holding and the cheek kissing the other day, it hasn't affected us in the bedroom. In fact, last night we moved past the slow and steady streak we've been on and played out a fantasy of mine that involved her Hooters uniform.

"You should try to get a job at Hooters," I tell Sydney. I know she's been looking for work, and even though it doesn't seem up her alley, the tips really are good.

"No, thanks," she says. "I wouldn't be caught dead in those shorts."

"They're actually very nice shorts. Soft. Stretchy. You'd be surprised. And last night when Bridgette was pretending she was serving me a platter of hot wings, I reached down and . . ."

"Warren," Sydney says. "Stop. I don't care. How many times do I have to tell you I don't care about your sex life?"

I frown. Ridge doesn't really like to hear about it, either, and I can't tell Bridgette because she's a part of the story and it would just be redundant. I miss Brennan. He always listened.

Bridgette's bedroom door opens, and I watch as her eyes search the living room for me. I can see a hint of a smile, but she's good at making sure I'm the only one who sees it.

"Good morning, Bridgette," I say to her. "Sleep well?"

Her eyes fall on Sydney, who's seated next to me on the couch again. She looks away, but not before I see a flash of hurt on her face.

"Screw you, Warren," Bridgette says, turning her attention toward the refrigerator.

Still, after holding hands and kissing my cheek, she thinks I'd ever mess with another girl?

I watch her as she slams stuff around in the kitchen, angrily. "I don't like how she's up your ass all the time," Bridgette says. I immediately turn to Sydney and laugh, because for one, she still thinks Sydney can't hear her, and two, I can't believe she just said that to me. If that isn't her laying claim to me, I don't know what is.

I love it.

"You think that's funny?" Bridgette says after spinning around. I quickly shake my head and lose my smile, but she throws her hand in Sydney's direction. "The girl obviously has it bad for you, and you can't even respect me enough to distance yourself from her until I'm out of the house?" She turns her back to us again. "First she gives Ridge some sob story so he'll let her move in, and now she's taking advantage of the fact that you know sign language so she can flirt with you."

I don't know who to feel worse for, Bridgette or Sydney. Or *myself*. "Bridgette, stop."

"*You* stop, Warren," she says, turning back around to face me. "Either stop crawling in bed with me at night or stop shacking up on the couch with *her* during the day."

I knew it was coming, but I hoped I wouldn't be here when it finally did.

Sydney reaches her breaking point and slaps her book against her thighs. "Bridgette, please!" she yells. "Shut up! Shut up, shut up, shut up! Christ! I don't know why you think I'm deaf, and I'm definitely not a whore and I'm not using sign language to flirt with Warren. I don't even know sign language. And from now on, please stop yelling when you speak to me!"

I'm scared to look at Bridgette. I feel torn, because I want to high-five Sydney for finally standing up for herself, but I want to hug Bridgette because I know this has to be hard for her. I suddenly feel like the prank was the worst prank in the history of pranks.

I glance up just in time to see a flood of hurt wash over Bridgette's face. She marches to her room and slams her door.

This is going to be impossible to fix. Sydney just single-handedly ruined my entire relationship with that outburst.

Okay, it wasn't all her. I played a huge part in it, too.

My chest hurts. I don't like this. I don't like the silence, and I don't like the fact that I'm about to have to go make this right. I put my hands on my knees and begin to stand. "Well, there goes my chance to act out all the role-playing scenes I've been imagining. Thanks a lot, Sydney."

She pushes her book off her lap and stands up. "Screw you, Warren."

Ouch. Double hurt.

Sydney walks over to Bridgette's bedroom door and knocks. After a few seconds, she cautiously slips inside and closes the door behind her.

If she somehow fixes this, I'll be indebted to her forever.

I sigh and run my hand through my hair, knowing this is my fault. I glance over at Ridge and he's staring at me. "What'd I miss?" he signs.

I slowly shake my head in shame. "Bridgette found out Sydney's not deaf and now Bridgette hates me. Sydney went to Bridgette's room to try and fix things because she feels guilty."

Confusion clouds Ridge's face. "Sydney?" he signs. "What does *she* have to feel guilty for?"

I shrug. "Going along with the prank, I guess. She feels bad that it embarrassed Bridgette."

Ridge shakes his head. "Bridgette deserved it. If anyone should be apologizing, it should be her. Not Sydney."

Why is he defending Sydney like he's her overprotective boyfriend? I glance at Bridgette's bedroom door, shocked that I actually hear a conversation going on in her room, rather than a catfight. Ridge waves his hand in the air to get my attention again.

"Bridgette isn't yelling at her, is she?" he signs. He looks worried, and frankly, that concerns me.

"You sure do seem to care a lot about Sydney's well-being," I sign.

His jaw tightens, and I know I probably shouldn't have

said anything. I can't help it, though. I've been through a lot with Ridge and Maggie, and I don't want him screwing things up just because he might find another girl attractive.

I can tell he doesn't want to take the conversation in that direction, so I redirect it back to me.

"No, neither of them are yelling," I sign. "But Bridgette *will* be as soon as she walks back out of her bedroom. She'll more than likely move out now, and I'll never be able to crawl out of bed again because . . ." I clasp my hand to my chest, "She's gonna take my heart with her."

He knows I'm being dramatic, so he rolls his eyes and laughs, turning to face his laptop again. The door to Bridgette's bedroom swings open, and she marches out.

I didn't prepare for this. I knew she'd be mad, but I'm not sure I can defend myself against her physically if we were in a real fight.

I sit up straight and watch in fear as she walks swiftly toward me. She kneels down onto the couch and slides her leg across my lap, straddling me.

I'm so confused.

Her hands meet my cheeks and she sighs. "I can't believe I'm falling in love with such a stupid, stupid asshole."

My heart wants to rejoice, but my mind is pulling on the reins.

Falling in love.

With an asshole.

A stupid, stupid asshole.

Holy shit! That's *me!*

I wrap my hands around her head and pull her mouth to mine at the same time that I stand up and begin making my way into my bedroom. I shut the door behind us and walk over to the bed and drop her on it. I take off my shirt and throw it on the floor.

"Say it again." I slide on top of her and she smiles, touching my face with the palms of her hands.

"I said I'm falling in love with you, Warren. I think. I'm pretty sure that's what this is."

I kiss her again, frantically. Those are the most beautiful words I've ever heard come out of another human. I pull back and look at her again. "But you wanted to kill me five minutes ago. What changed?" I lift up onto my hands. "Did Sydney pay you to say that? Is this a prank?" My heart stops. Bridgette shakes her head.

I would die. I would literally die if she took them back. I would die so much better than Brody dies, because my death would be *actual* death.

"I just . . ." Bridgette pauses, searching for the right words. "I've been thinking this whole time that maybe you were messing around with Sydney. But after talking to her, I know that's not true. And she also mentioned that one night when you were drunk, you said you might love me. And that just . . . I don't know, Warren."

God, I love this. I love her nervousness. I love her hesitation. I love that she's talking to me so openly. "Tell me, Bridgette," I say quietly, urging her to finish what she was saying. I roll onto my side and lift up onto my elbow. I brush the hair away from her forehead and lean forward to kiss it.

"When she said that, it made me feel . . . *happy*. And I realized that I'm never happy. I was an unhappy child and I'm an unhappy adult and nothing in my life makes me feel the way you do. So I just . . . I think that's what this feeling is. I think I'm falling in love with you."

A small droplet of a tear escapes from the corner of her eye, and as much as I want to bottle it up and save it for all of eternity, I pretend not to notice it, because I know that's what she would prefer. I kiss her lips again before pulling back and looking her directly in the eyes. "I'm falling in love with you, too."

She smiles and reaches her hand up to the back of my head, slowly pulling my mouth to hers. She kisses me softly and then gently pushes me onto my back. She eases herself on top of me and presses her hands against my chest.

"I think I should clarify that I never said I was *in* love with you. I just said I was *falling* in love with you. There's a difference."

I grab her by the hips and pull her closer. "The only difference between *falling* in love and *being* in love is that your heart already knows how you feel, but your mind is too stubborn to admit it." Then I whisper in her ear. "But take all the time you need. I have nothing but patience for you."

"Good, because I'm not telling you I love you yet. Because I don't. I might be on my way to that point, but anything could derail that."

I can't help but smile and kiss her after that little disclaimer.

After a few more minutes of kissing, she turns her head to the side and holds up a finger, silently asking me to stop. She pulls away and sits up on the bed, hugging her knees. She lays her head on her arms and squeezes her eyes shut.

She's quiet for several moments, and her reaction is unusual for her. She looks guilty. She doesn't ever look guilty because she's always too angry to feel any sense of guilt.

"What's the matter?" I ask her.

She quickly shakes her head. "I'm the worst person in the world," she whispers. She turns her head toward mine, slowly. I don't like the look on her face.

She begins to scoot off the bed and I feel my heart dragging behind her. "It was a prank, Warren," she says softly as she stands.

I rise up onto my elbows. "What do you mean?"

She turns to face me and her eyes are so full of shame, she can't even look at me without wincing. "I was trying to get back at you for letting me think Sydney was deaf." She opens the bathroom door and looks down at her feet. "I said all that because I was mad at you, not because it's really how I feel. I'm not falling in love with you, Warren."

I think you're standing on my heart, Bridgette.

She glances over her shoulder into the bathroom, and then back at me. "I didn't mean to take it that far. This is really awkward. I'm gonna go back to my room now." She closes the door behind her.

I'm too numb to feel. Too numb to move. Too numb to process the words that just came out of her mouth. My throat hurts, my stomach hurts, my chest hurts, even my fucking lungs hurt and *oh, my God*, it hurts so much.

I fall back to the bed and bring two fists to my forehead.

"Hey, Warren," she says from the doorway.

I look up at her and she still looks just as guilty. She waves her hand back and forth between us. "That whole thing that just happened? That was . . ." Her frown transforms into a shit-eating grin. "*That* was actually the prank!"

She runs and jumps on the bed, and begins dancing around me. "You should have seen your face!" She's laughing and jumping, bouncing every aching part of me up and down on the bed.

I want to kill her.

She falls to her knees and leans over me, pressing her lips to mine. When she pulls back, I don't want to kill her anymore. My whole body is miraculously healed by her smile. I feel better than I've ever felt. I feel stronger, more alive, happier, and somehow more in love with her than I was five minutes ago. I pull her against me. "That was a really good prank, Bridgette."

She laughs. "I know. It was the best."

I nod. "It really was."

I hold her for several quiet minutes, replaying the entire scene in my head. "God, you're such a bitch."

She laughs again. "I know. A bitch who finally met the right asshole."

Chapter Eleven

Guess who woke up in Bridgette's bed again this morning?

Me.

And guess who'll be falling asleep in Bridgette's bed to-night?

That's right. *Me.*

Both of those things are great, but not as great as this moment. Right now.

We're both seated on the couch, and she's lying between my legs with her head on my chest. We're watching a movie where the actors actually stay dressed for the entire film. But it's not really important what film it is, because Bridgette's cuddling with me.

This is a first, and it's incredible, and I love how she makes me appreciate such simple, mundane things.

Both of us glance at the door when we hear a key being inserted into the lock. The door opens and Brennan walks in. I immediately sit up on the couch, because he's supposed to be in Dallas tonight. He has a show tomorrow, and I'm positive I booked him a hotel for the right night.

Bridgette sits up on the couch and looks at him. He smiles at her, but it's a forced smile. He reaches for his back pocket and pulls out a sheet of paper. He holds it up. "This came today," he says.

Bridgette squeezes my hand and that's when I realize he's holding the test results. I've known Brennan long enough to know by his reaction that he's not happy about the results. I just don't know if that's a good thing or a bad thing for Bridgette.

"Just tell me," she whispers.

Brennan looks down at his feet and then up to me. The look in his eyes is enough for Bridgette to know that she's not any closer to figuring out who her real father is than she was a few months ago.

She inhales a deep breath, and then stands up. She mutters a "thank you" to Brennan and begins heading toward her bedroom, but he grabs her by the arm and pulls her to him. He wraps his arms around her and gives her a hug, but in true Bridgette fashion, she doesn't allow it to last more than two seconds. She begins to cry, and I know that Bridgette doesn't want anyone to see her cry. She ducks her head and rushes to her room.

Brennan tosses the paper on the counter and runs his hands through his hair. "This sucks, man," he says. "I felt like she really needed it to be true, and instead, it just adds to all the shit she's had to deal with her whole life."

I sigh and drop my head against the couch. "You sure about the results? There's no way they could have messed up?"

Brennan shakes his head. "She's not his daughter. And in a way, I'm happy for her because who would want him for a dad? But I know she liked the idea of finally having a little bit of closure."

I stand up and squeeze the back of my neck. "I don't think closure is the only thing she was hoping for." I point to her bedroom. "I'm gonna go check on her," I tell him. "Thanks for coming all this way to tell her."

Brennan nods, and I make my way into her bedroom. She's curled up on the far side of her bed, facing opposite from the door.

I'm not good at consoling, so I'm not sure what I can say to make her feel any better. Instead, I just climb onto the bed and scoot in behind her. I wrap my arm over her and grab her hand.

We lie like this for several minutes, and I let her get all her tears out. When it doesn't sound like she's crying anymore, I press a kiss into her hair.

"He would have been a horrible father, Bridgette."

She nods. "I know. I just . . ." She sucks in a rush of air. "I like it here. I feel like all of you accept me for who I am, and that's never happened before. And now that Brennan knows I'm not his sister, what happens now? Do I just leave?"

I squeeze her tighter, hating that she even thinks that's an option. "Over my and Brody's dead bodies. No way am I letting you go anywhere."

She laughs and wipes at her eyes. "You guys don't have to be nice to me out of pity."

I roll her onto her back and shake my head in confusion. "Pity? This isn't pity, Bridgette. I mean, yeah, I feel bad for you. Yeah, it might have been cool if you were their sister. But it doesn't change anything. The only thing those test results would have changed is that you'd go from not knowing who your real father is to having one of the worst fathers in the world." I kiss her on the forehead. "I don't care whose sister you are, I love you the same."

Her eyes widen, and I can feel her body stiffen in my arms. I didn't say I was falling in love this time.

I just told her I loved her. Like, actively. And yes, those three words could probably make her flip out more than any other three words in the English language, but I can't take it back. I *won't* take it back. I love her, and I've loved her for months now and I'm tired of being too scared of her reaction to say it.

She begins to shake her head. "Warren . . ."

"I know," I interject. "I said it. Get over it. I love you, Bridgette."

Her expression is void of any emotion right now. She's absorbing it. She's waiting to see how those words make her feel, because I'm not sure if she's ever heard them before.

Her jaw grows tense, and she places her hands against my chest. "You're a liar," she snaps, attempting to roll out from under me.

Here we go again.

I pull her back to the mattress while she attempts to squirm away. "You're exhausting, you know that?" I roll her onto her back and she begins to nod, frantically.

"That's right, Warren. I'm exhausting. I'm mean. I always see the glass half empty, and if you think telling me you love me will make me nicer and less exhausting, you're wrong. You can't change me. Everyone wants to change me, but I am who I am, and if you think me telling you that I love you, too, will make me shit out unicorns and rainbows, you're wrong. I *hate* unicorns and rainbows."

I drop my face to her neck and I start to laugh. "*Oh, my God,* I can't believe you're mine." I kiss her on the cheek, and then I kiss her on the forehead, and then her nose and her chin and her other cheek. I look back at her eyes full of confusion.

"I don't *want* you to change, Bridgette. I'm not in love with who you *could* be, or who you *used* to be, or who the world *says* you should be. I'm in love with *you*. Right now. Just like this."

She's still guarded and defensive, so I pull her closer to me and wrap my arms around her, hugging her tightly. "Stop," I whisper in her ear. "Stop telling yourself that you aren't lovable, because it's pissing me off. I don't care if you aren't ready to admit how you really feel about me yet, but don't you dare dismiss how I feel about you. Because I love you." I kiss her on the side of the head, and I say it again. It feels so good to finally say it. "I love you, Bridgette."

She pulls away just enough for me to see her face. Her eyes are rimmed with tears.

"Bridgette, I love you," I say again, this time looking her straight in the eyes. I can feel her struggling internally. Part of her wants to enjoy this moment, and part of her is trying to hold up that last wall that still stands between us.

"I love you," I whisper again.

One of the tears escapes from her eyes, and I'm afraid she's about to break and push me away like she always does. I press my lips against hers, and I inhale deeply. I touch her cheek and wipe away her tear with my thumb.

"You're the most genuine person I know, Bridgette. So whether you think you deserve love or not, it doesn't matter, because I can't help it. I fell in love with you, and I'm not sorry for it."

Another tear falls from her eyes.

A smile forms on her lips.

A laugh escapes her mouth, and her chest begins to shake because she's laughing and crying and kissing me. And I kiss her right back, crashing right through the last wall that stood between us.

She wraps her hands in my hair and rolls me onto my back, still with her lips pressed to mine. I open my eyes and she backs away from my mouth, still smiling. She begins to shake her head in slow disbelief. "I can't believe I'm in love with such a stupid, stupid asshole."

I'm not sure this sentence could mean more to any other man in the world.

"I love you, Warren."

I can't even tell her I love her back, because hearing those words come out of her mouth has left me completely speechless. But I don't think she cares, because her lips are on mine so hard and fast, I wouldn't be able to speak anyway.

I'm in love with Bridgette.

Bridgette is in love with me.

All is finally right in the world.

We continue to kiss while we remove each other's clothes. Neither one of us is in control this time. She makes love to me at the same time I make love to her, and no one is in charge. No one is calling the shots. It's completely equal now. She feels about me how I feel about her and when we're finished, she whispers, "I love you, Warren."

And I say, "I love you, Bridgette."

And no one argues.

She lies peacefully in my arms and doesn't try to kick me

out of her bed. Just the thought of having to go back to my room and sleep alone seems ridiculous, and I'm not sure I ever want to sleep alone again.

I stroke her arm with my fingers. "I have an idea," I whisper against her hair.

She shakes her head. "I'm not doing anal."

I laugh and pull back. "*What?* No. Not that. Not yet, anyway." I push her off me and sit up, pulling her to a seated position. I take both of her hands in mine, and I look her very seriously in the eyes. "I think we should move in together."

Her eyes widen in shock and she's looking at me like I've lost my mind. Maybe I have. "We already live together, dumbass. And we hardly have to pay rent. We'd be broke if we got our own place."

I dismiss her concerns with a shake of my head. "I don't mean into a new apartment. Move into my bedroom with me. We're together every night anyway."

She's still shaking her head. "Why would I want to do that?"

"Because," I say to her, brushing her hair behind her ear. "It's romantic."

"No, Warren, it's dumb."

I fall back onto the bed, frustrated. She drops to my side and glares down at me. "Why would I want to move all my clothes into your tiny closet? That's so stupid. I have way too much closet stuff."

"Fine," I tell her. "You can keep all your clothes in your own closet, but move everything else into my room."

She drops her forehead to my chest. "I don't *have* any other stuff. I have a bed. That's it."

I tuck my finger under her chin and lift her eyes to mine. "Exactly. Move your bed to my room. We both have full-size beds. Putting them together would be like having a king, and we'd have more room to have sex, and when we're finished you can roll over to your side of the bed and I can watch you sleep."

She considers my proposal for several quiet moments, and then smiles. "This is so dumb."

I sit up and pull her off the bed. "And romantic. Come on, get dressed. I'll help you."

We put our clothes back on and begin tossing the blankets and pillows off her bed. We lift the mattress and begin scooting it out the door, into the living room, and toward my room. Ridge and Brennan are both sitting on the couch, staring at us.

"What the hell are you doing?" Brennan asks.

I press my hip against the mattress so I can sign back to them. "Bridgette and I are moving in together."

Ridge and Brennan look at each other, then back at me. "But . . . you already *live* together," Brennan says.

I dismiss them with a wave of my hand, and we finish moving Bridgette's mattress next to mine. Once her bed is remade, she falls onto hers and I onto mine. We roll until we're facing each other. She rests her head on her arm and sighs.

"We've lived together for two minutes, and I'm already sick of your face."

I laugh. "I think you should move out. We got along so much better before this."

She flips me off, so I grab her hand and link my fingers through hers. "I need to ask you something else."

She falls onto her back. "So help me God, Warren, if you ask me to marry you I'll cut your nuts off."

"I don't want to marry you," I say. "Yet. But . . ."

I crawl over to her part of our home and lie next to her. "Will you go on a date with me?"

She looks away from me and stares up at the ceiling. "Oh, my God," she whispers. "We've never been on a date before?"

"Not a real one."

She slaps a hand to her forehead. "I'm such a whore. I already moved in with you and we haven't even been on a date?"

"You're not a whore," I say to her with mock reassurance. "We haven't even had sex . . . *oh, wait.*" I grimace. "You *are* such a whore. A huge, slutty whore who wants me to try anal with her tonight."

She laughs and shoves me in the chest.

I shove her back.

She shoves me harder.

I push her until she's at the edge of her bed.

She lifts her legs to kick me.

I kick her back, pushing her off the bed until she's lying on the floor. After several quiet seconds, I scoot to the edge of the mattress and look down at her. She's still lying flat on her back in the same position she landed.

"You could give Brody a run for his money," I tell her. She reaches up a hand to hit me, but I grab it and pull it to my mouth. I kiss the top of it and hold her hand while I lock eyes with her.

She's in an unusually agreeable mood right now, which leads me to believe that maybe . . . *just maybe* . . .

"I have one more question, Bridgette."

She cocks an eyebrow and slowly shakes her head. "I'm not telling you the name of that porn."

I drop her hand and roll onto my back. "Fuck."

Maybe not.

Acknowledgments

A huge thank-you to so many people. First, my family. Without you I could never finish anything. To my publisher, Atria Books, and Judith Curr, for not saying no when I said, "I want to write a novella about Warren. And I want it to be a surprise!" A special thanks to my editor, Johanna Castillo, for being the absolute best! I say it with every book, but we really are a great team. To my brand-new publicist, Ariele, for being top-notch at her job. Yer er der berst, Erererl! And to my agent, Jane Dystel, and her team of amazing people. To Murphy and Stephanie for always keeping my head above water. And last but not least, my readers. Without you, none of the people just mentioned would have a job, including me. Your passion for reading gives us the ability to live our passion. For that, we ALL thank you!

Enjoy an excerpt from Colleen Hoover's
Maybe Someday, **the novel that inspired the**
characters in *Maybe Not*

prologue

Sydney

I just punched a girl in the face. Not just *any* girl. My best friend. My roommate.

Well, as of five minutes ago, I guess I should call her my *ex*-roommate.

Her nose began bleeding almost immediately, and for a second, I felt bad for hitting her. But then I remembered what a lying, betraying whore she is, and it made me want to punch her again. I would have if Hunter hadn't prevented it by stepping between us.

So instead, I punched *him*. I didn't do any damage to him, unfortunately. Not like the damage I'd done to my hand.

Punching someone hurts a lot worse than I imagined it would. Not that I spend an excessive amount of time imagining how it would feel to punch people. Although I am having that urge again as I stare down at my phone at the incoming text from Ridge. He's another one I'd like to get even with. I know he technically has nothing to do with my current predicament, but he could have given me a heads-up a little sooner. Therefore, I'd like to punch him, too.

Of course, I don't want to come up. My fist hurts enough as it is, and if I went up to Ridge's apartment, it would hurt a whole lot worse after I finished with him.

I turn around and look up at his balcony. He's leaning against his sliding-glass door; phone in hand, watching me. It's almost dark, but the lights from the courtyard illuminate his face. His dark eyes lock with mine, and the way his mouth curls up into a soft, regretful smile makes it hard to remember why I'm even upset with him in the first place. He runs a free hand through the hair hanging loosely over his forehead, revealing even more of the worry in his expression. Or maybe that's a look of regret. As it should be.

I decide not to reply and flip him off instead. He shakes his head and shrugs his shoulders, as if to say, *I tried*, and then he goes back inside his apartment and slides his door shut.

I put the phone back in my pocket before it gets wet, and I look around at the courtyard of the apartment complex where I've lived for two whole months. When we first moved in, the hot Texas summer was swallowing up the last traces of spring, but this courtyard seemed to somehow still cling to life. Vibrant blue and purple hydrangeas lined the walkways leading up to the staircases, and the fountain affixed in the center of the courtyard.

Now that summer has reached its most unattractive peak, the water in the fountain has long since evaporated. The hydrangeas are a sad, wilted reminder of the excitement

I felt when Tori and I first moved in here. Looking at the courtyard now, defeated by the season, is an eerie parallel to how I feel at the moment. Defeated and sad.

I'm sitting on the edge of the now empty cement fountain, my elbows propped up on the two suitcases that contain most of my belongings, waiting for a cab to pick me up. I have no idea where it's going to take me, but I know I'd rather be anywhere except where I am right now. Which is, well, homeless.

I could call my parents, but that would give them ammunition to start firing all the *We told you sos* at me.

We told you not to move so far away, Sydney.

We told you not to get serious with that guy.

We told you if you had chosen prelaw over music, we would have paid for it.

We told you to punch with your thumb on the outside *of your fist.*

Okay, maybe they never taught me the proper punching techniques, but if they're so right all the damn time, they *should* have.

I clench my fist, then spread out my fingers, then clench it again. My hand is surprisingly sore, and I'm pretty sure I should put ice on it. I feel sorry for guys. Punching sucks.

Know what else sucks? Rain. It always finds the most inappropriate time to fall, like right now, while I'm homeless.

The cab finally pulls up, and I stand and grab my suitcases. I roll them behind me as the cab driver gets out and pops open the trunk. Before I even hand him the first suitcase, my heart sinks as I suddenly realize that I don't even have my purse on me.

Shit.

I look around, back to where I was sitting on the suitcases, then feel around my body as if my purse will magically appear across my shoulder. But I know exactly where my purse is. I pulled it off my shoulder and dropped it to the floor right before I punched Tori in her overpriced, Cameron Diaz nose.

I sigh. And I laugh. Of course, I left my purse. My first day of being homeless would have been way too easy if I'd had a purse with me.

"I'm sorry," I say to the cab driver, who is now loading my second piece of luggage. "I changed my mind. I don't need a cab right now."

I know there's a hotel about a half-mile from here. If I can just work up the courage to go back inside and get my purse, I'll walk there and get a room until I figure out what to do. It's not as if I can get any wetter.

The driver takes the suitcases back out of the cab, sets them on the curb in front of me, and walks back to the driver's side without ever making eye contact. He just gets into his car and drives away, as if my canceling is a relief.

Do I look that pathetic?

I take my suitcases and walk back to where I was seated before I realized I was purseless. I glance up to my apartment and wonder what would happen if I went back there to get my wallet. I sort of left things in a mess when I walked out the door. I guess I'd rather be homeless in the rain than go back up there.

I take a seat on my luggage again and contemplate my situation. I could pay someone to go upstairs for me. But who? No one's outside, and who's to say Hunter or Tori would even give the person my purse?

This really sucks. I know I'm going to have to end up calling one of my friends, but right now, I'm too embarrassed to tell anyone how clueless I've been for the last two years. I've been completely blindsided.

I already hate being twenty-two, and I still have 364 more days to go.

It sucks so bad that I'm . . . *crying*?

Great. I'm crying now. I'm a purseless, crying, violent, homeless girl. And as much as I don't want to admit it, I think I might also be heartbroken.

Yep. Sobbing now. Pretty sure this must be what it feels like to have your heart broken.

"It's raining. Hurry up."

I glance up to see a girl hovering over me. She's holding an umbrella over her head and looking down at me with agitation while she hops from one foot to the other, waiting for me to do something. "I'm getting soaked. *Hurry.*"

Her voice is a little demanding, as if she's doing me some sort of favor and I'm being ungrateful. I arch an eyebrow as I look up at her, shielding the rain from my eyes with my hand. I don't know why she's complaining about getting wet, when there isn't much clothing to *get* wet. She's wearing next to nothing. I glance at her shirt, which is missing its entire bottom half, and realize she's in a Hooters outfit.

Could this day get any weirder? I'm sitting on almost everything I own in a torrential downpour, being bossed around by a bitchy Hooters waitress.

I'm still staring at her shirt when she grabs my hand and

pulls me up in a huff. "Ridge said you would do this. I've got to get to work. Follow me, and I'll show you where the apartment is." She grabs one of my suitcases, pops the handle out, and shoves it at me. She takes the other and walks swiftly out of the courtyard. I follow her, for no other reason than the fact that she's taken one of my suitcases with her and I want it back.

She yells over her shoulder as she begins to ascend the stairwell. "I don't know how long you plan on staying, but I've only got one rule. Stay the hell out of my room."

She reaches an apartment and opens the door, never even looking back to see if I'm following her. Once I reach the top of the stairs, I pause outside the apartment and look down at the fern sitting unaffected by the heat in a planter outside the door. Its leaves are lush and green as if they're giving summer the middle finger with their refusal to succumb to the heat. I smile at the plant, somewhat proud of it. Then I frown with the realization that I'm envious of the resilience of a plant.

I shake my head, look away, then take a hesitant step inside the unfamiliar apartment. The layout is similar to my own apartment, only this one is a double split bedroom with four total bedrooms. My and Tori's apartment only had two bedrooms, but the living rooms are the same size.

The only other noticeable difference is that I don't see any lying, backstabbing, bloody-nosed whores standing in this one. Nor do I see any of Tori's dirty dishes or laundry lying around.

The girl sets my suitcase down beside the door, then steps aside and waits for me to . . . well, I don't know what she's waiting for me to do.

She rolls her eyes and grabs my arm, pulling me out of the doorway and further into the apartment. "What the hell is wrong with you? Do you even speak?" She begins to close the door behind her but pauses and turns around, wide-eyed. She holds her finger up in the air. "Wait," she says. "You're not . . ." She rolls her eyes and smacks herself in the forehead. "Oh, my God, you're deaf."

Huh? What the hell is wrong with this girl? I shake my head and start to answer her, but she interrupts me.

"God, Bridgette," she mumbles to herself. She rubs her hands down her face and groans, completely ignoring the fact that I'm shaking my head. "You're such an insensitive bitch sometimes."

Wow. This girl has some serious issues in the people-skills department. She's sort of a bitch, even though she's making an effort not to be one. Now that she thinks I'm deaf. I don't even know how to respond. She shakes her head as if she's disappointed in herself, then looks straight at me.

"I . . . HAVE . . . TO . . . GO . . . TO . . . WORK . . . NOW!" she yells very loudly and painfully slowly. I grimace and step back, which should be a huge clue that I can hear her practically yelling, but she doesn't notice. She points to a door at the end of the hallway. "RIDGE . . . IS . . . IN . . . HIS . . . ROOM!"

Before I have a chance to tell her she can stop yelling, she leaves the apartment and closes the door behind her.

I have no idea what to think. Or what to do now. I'm standing, soaking wet, in the middle of an unfamiliar apartment, and the only person besides Hunter and Tori whom I feel like punching is now just a few feet away in another room. And speaking of Ridge, why the hell did he send his psycho Hooters girlfriend to get me? I take out my phone and have begun to text him when his bedroom door opens.

He walks out into the hallway with an armful of blankets and a pillow. As soon as he makes eye contact with me, I gasp. I hope it's not a noticeable gasp. It's just that I've never actually seen him up close before, and he's even better-looking from just a few feet away than he is from across an apartment building's courtyard.

I don't think I've ever seen eyes that can actually speak. I'm not sure what I mean by that. It just seems as if he could shoot me the tiniest glance with those dark eyes of his, and I'd know exactly what they needed me to do. They're piercing and intense and—oh, my God, I'm staring.

The corner of his mouth tilts up in a knowing smile as he passes me and heads straight for the couch.

Despite his appealing and slightly innocent-looking face, I want to yell at him for being so deceitful. He shouldn't have waited more than two weeks to tell me. I would have had a chance to plan all this out a little better. I don't understand how we could have had two weeks' worth of conversations without his feeling the need to tell me that my boyfriend and my best friend were screwing.

Ridge throws the blankets and the pillow onto the couch.

"I'm not staying here, Ridge," I say, attempting to stop him from wasting time with his hospitality. I know he feels bad for me, but I hardly know him, and I'd feel a lot more comfortable in a hotel room than sleeping on a strange couch.

Then again, hotel rooms require money.

Something I don't have on me at the moment.

Something that's inside my purse, across the courtyard,

in an apartment with the only two people in the world I don't want to see right now.

Maybe a couch isn't such a bad idea after all.

He gets the couch made up and turns around, dropping his eyes to my soaking-wet clothes. I look down at the puddle of water I'm creating in the middle of his floor.

"Oh, sorry," I mutter. My hair is matted to my face; my shirt is now a see-through pathetic excuse for a barrier between the outside world and my very pink, very noticeable bra. "Where's your bathroom?"

He nods his head toward the bathroom door.

I turn around, unzip a suitcase, and begin to rummage through it while Ridge walks back into his bedroom. I'm glad he doesn't ask me questions about what happened after our conversation earlier. I'm not in the mood to talk about it.

I select a pair of yoga pants and a tank top, then grab my bag of toiletries and head to the bathroom. It disturbs me that everything about this apartment reminds me of my own, with just a few subtle differences. This is the same bathroom with the Jack-and-Jill doors on the left and right, leading to the two bedrooms that adjoin it. One is Ridge's, obviously. I'm curious about who the other bedroom belongs to but not curious enough to open it. The Hooters girl's one rule was to stay the hell out of her room, and she doesn't seem like the type to kid around.

I shut the door that leads to the living room and lock it, then check the locks on both doors to the bedrooms to make sure no one can walk in. I have no idea if anyone lives in this apartment other than Ridge and the Hooters girl, but I don't want to chance it.

I pull off my sopping clothes and throw them into the sink to avoid soaking the floor. I turn on the shower and wait until the water gets warm, then step in. I stand under the stream of water and close my eyes, thankful that I'm not still sitting outside in the rain. At the same time, I'm not really happy to be where I am, either.

I never expected my twenty-second birthday to end with me showering in a strange apartment and sleeping on a couch that belongs to a guy I've barely known for two weeks, all at the hands of the two people I cared about and trusted the most.

1.

Sydney

I slide open my balcony door and step outside, thankful that the sun has already dipped behind the building next door, cooling the air to what could pass as a perfect fall temperature. Almost on cue, the sound of his guitar floats across the courtyard as I take a seat and lean back into the patio lounger. I tell Tori I come out here to get homework done, because I don't want to admit that the guitar is the only reason I'm outside every night at eight, like clockwork.

For weeks now, the guy in the apartment across the courtyard has sat on his balcony and played for at least an hour. Every night, I sit outside and listen.

I've noticed a few other neighbors come out to their balconies when he's playing, but no one is as loyal as I am. I don't understand how someone could hear these songs and not crave them day after day. Then again, music has always been a passion of mine, so maybe I'm just a little more infatuated with his sound than other people are. I've played the piano for as long as I can remember, and although I've never shared it with anyone, I love writing music. I even switched my major to music education two years ago. My plan is to be an elementary music teacher, although if my father had his way, I'd still be prelaw.

"A life of mediocrity is a waste of a life," he said when I informed him that I was changing my major.

A life of mediocrity. I find that more amusing than insulting, since he seems to be the most dissatisfied person I've ever known. And he's a lawyer. Go figure.

One of the familiar songs ends and the guy with the guitar begins to play something he's never played before. I've grown accustomed to his unofficial playlist since he seems to practice the same songs in the same order night after night. However, I've never heard him play this particular song before. The way he's repeating the same chords makes me think he's creating the song right here on the spot. I like that I'm witnessing this, especially since after only a few chords, it's already my new favorite. All his songs sound like originals. I wonder if he performs them locally or if he just writes them for fun.

I lean forward in the chair, rest my arms on the edge of the balcony, and watch him. His balcony is directly across the courtyard, far enough away that I don't feel weird when I watch him but close enough that I make sure I'm never watching him when Hunter's around. I don't think Hunter would like the fact that I've developed a tiny crush on this guy's talent.

I can't deny it, though. Anyone who watches how passionately this guy plays would crush on his talent. The way he keeps his eyes closed the entire time, focusing intently on every stroke against every guitar string. I like it best when he sits cross-legged with the guitar upright between his legs. He pulls it against his chest and plays it like a stand-up bass, keeping his eyes closed the whole time. It's so mesmerizing to watch him that sometimes I catch myself holding my breath, and I don't even realize I'm doing it until I'm gasping for air.

It also doesn't help that he's cute. At least, he seems cute from here. His light brown hair is unruly and moves with him, falling across his forehead every time he looks down at his guitar. He's too far away to distinguish eye color or distinct features, but the details don't matter when coupled with the passion he has for his music. There's a confidence to him that I find compelling. I've always admired musicians who are able to tune out everyone and everything around them and pour all of their focus into their music. To be able to shut the world off and allow yourself to be completely swept away is something I've always wanted the confidence to do, but I just don't have it.

This guy has it. He's confident and talented. I've always been a sucker for musicians, but more in a fantasy way. They're a different breed. A breed that rarely makes for good boyfriends.

He glances at me as if he can hear my thoughts, and then a slow grin appears across his face. He never once pauses the song while he continues to watch me. The eye contact makes me blush, so I drop my arms and pull my notebook back onto my lap and look down at it. I hate that he just caught me staring so hard. Not that I was doing anything wrong; it just feels odd for him to know I was watching him. I glance up again, and he's still watching me, but he's not smiling anymore. The way he's staring causes my heart to speed up, so I look away and focus on my notebook.

Way to be a creeper, Sydney.

"There's my girl," a comforting voice says from behind me. I lean my head back and tilt my eyes upward to watch Hunter as he makes his way onto the balcony. I try to hide the fact that I'm shocked to see him, because I'm pretty sure I was supposed to remember he was coming.

On the off chance that Guitar Boy is still watching, I make it a point to seem really into Hunter's hello kiss so that maybe I'll seem less like a creepy stalker and more like someone just casually relaxing on her balcony. I run my hand up Hunter's neck as he leans over the back of my chair and kisses me upside down.

"Scoot up," Hunter says, pushing on my shoulders. I do what he asks and slide forward in the seat as he lifts his leg over the chair and slips in behind me. He pulls my back against his chest and wraps his arms around me.

My eyes betray me when the sound of the guitar stops abruptly, and I glance across the courtyard once more. Guitar Boy is eyeing us hard as he stands, then goes back inside his apartment. His expression is odd. Almost angry.

"How was school?" Hunter asks.

"Too boring to talk about. What about you? How was work?"

"Interesting," he says, brushing my hair away from my neck with his hand. He presses his lips to my neck and kisses his way down my collarbone.

"What was so interesting?"

He tightens his hold on me, then rests his chin on my

shoulder and pulls me back in the chair with him. "The oddest thing happened at lunch," he says. "I was with one of the guys at this Italian restaurant. We were eating out on the patio, and I had just asked the waiter what he recommended for dessert, when a police car rounded the corner. They stopped right in front of the restaurant, and two officers jumped out with their guns drawn. They began barking orders toward us when our waiter mumbled, 'Shit.' He slowly raised his hands, and the police jumped the barrier to the patio, rushed toward him, threw him to the ground, and cuffed him right at our feet. After they read him his rights, they pulled him to his feet and escorted him toward the cop car. The waiter glanced back at me and yelled, 'The tiramisu is really good!' Then they put him in the car and drove away."

I tilt my head back and look up at him. "Seriously? That really happened?"

He nods, laughing. "I swear, Syd. It was crazy."

"Well? Did you try the tiramisu?"

"Hell, yeah, we did. It was the best tiramisu I've ever had." He kisses me on the cheek and pushes me forward. "Speaking of food, I'm starving." He stands up and holds out his hand to me. "Did you cook tonight?"

I take his hand and let him pull me up. "We just had salad, but I can make you one."

Once we're inside, Hunter takes a seat on the couch next to Tori. She's got a textbook spread open across her lap as she halfheartedly focuses on both homework and TV at the same time. I take out the containers from the fridge and make his salad. I feel a little guilty that I forgot tonight was one of the nights he said he was coming. I usually have something cooked when I know he'll be here.

We've been dating for almost two years now. I met him during my sophomore year in college, when he was a senior. He and Tori had been friends for years. After she moved into my dorm and we became friends, she insisted I meet him. She said we'd hit it off, and she was right. We made it official after only two dates, and things have been wonderful since.

Of course, we have our ups and downs, especially since he moved more than an hour away. When he landed the job in the accounting firm last semester, he suggested I move with him. I told him no, that I really wanted to finish my undergrad before taking such a huge step. In all honesty, I'm just scared.

The thought of moving in with him seems so final, as if I would be sealing my fate. I know that once we take that step, the next step is marriage, and then I'd be looking at never having the chance to live alone. I've always had a roommate, and until I can afford my own place, I'll be sharing an apartment with Tori. I haven't told Hunter yet, but I really want to live alone for a year. It's something I promised myself I would do before I got married. I don't even turn twenty-two for a couple of weeks, so it's not as if I'm in any hurry.

I take Hunter's food to him in the living room.

"Why do you watch this?" he says to Tori. "All these women do is talk shit about each other and flip tables."

"That's exactly why I watch it," Tori says, without taking her eyes off the TV.

Hunter winks at me and takes his food, then props his feet up on the coffee table. "Thanks, babe." He turns toward the TV and begins eating. "Can you grab me a beer?"

I nod and walk back into the kitchen. I open the refrigerator door and look on the shelf where he always keeps his extra beer. I realize as I'm staring at "his" shelf that this is probably how it begins. First, he has a shelf in the refrigerator. Then he'll have a toothbrush in the bathroom, a drawer in my dresser, and eventually his stuff will infiltrate mine in so many ways it'll be impossible for me ever to be on my own.

I run my hands up my arms, rubbing away the sudden onset of discomfort washing over me. I feel as if I'm watching my future play out in front of me. I'm not so sure I like what I'm imagining.

Am I ready for this?

Am I ready for this guy to be the guy I bring dinner to every night when he gets home from work?

Am I ready to fall into this comfortable life with him? One where I teach all day and he does people's taxes, and then we come home and I cook dinner and I "grab him beers" while he props his feet up and calls me *babe*, and then we go to our bed and make love at approximately nine P.M. so we won't be tired the next day, in order to wake up and get dressed and go to work and do it all over again?

"Earth to Sydney," Hunter says. I hear him snap his fingers twice. "Beer? Please, babe?"

I quickly grab his beer, give it to him, then head straight to my bathroom. I turn the water on in the shower, but I don't get in. Instead, I lock the door and sink to the floor.

We have a good relationship. He's good to me, and I know he loves me. I just don't understand why every time I think about a future with him, it's not an exciting thought.

Ridge

Maggie leans forward and kisses my forehead. "I need to go."

I'm on my back with my head and shoulders partially propped against my headboard. She's straddling my lap and looking down at me regretfully. I hate that we live so far apart now, but it makes the time we do spend together a lot more meaningful. I take her hands so she'll shut up, and I pull her to me, hoping to persuade her not to leave just yet.

She laughs and shakes her head. She kisses me, but only briefly, and then she pulls away again. She slides off my lap, but I don't let her make it very far before I lunge forward and pin her to the mattress. I point to her chest.

"You"—I lean in and kiss the tip of her nose—"need to stay one more night."

"I can't. I have class."

I grab her wrists and pin her arms above her head, then press my lips to hers. I know she won't stay another night. She's never missed a day of class in her life, unless she was too sick to move. I sort of wish she was feeling a little sick right now, so I could make her stay in bed with me.

I slide my hands from her wrists, delicately up her arms until I'm cupping her face. Then I give her one final kiss before I reluctantly pull away from her. "Go. And be careful. Let me know when you make it home."

She nods and pushes herself off the bed. She reaches

across me and grabs her shirt, then pulls it on over her head. I watch her as she walks around the room and gathers the clothes I pulled off her in a hurry.

After five years of dating, most couples would have moved in together by now. However, most peoples' other halves aren't Maggie. She's so fiercely independent it's almost intimidating. But it's understandable, considering how her life has gone. She's been caring for her grandfather since I met her. Before that, she spent the majority of her teenage years helping him care for her grandmother, who died when Maggie was sixteen. Now that her grandfather is in a nursing home, she finally has a chance to live alone while finishing school, and as much as I want her here with me, I also know how important this internship is for her. So for the next year, I'll suck it up while she's in San Antonio and I'm here in Austin. I'll be damned if I ever move out of Austin, especially for San Antonio.

Unless she asked, of course.

"Tell your brother I said good luck." She's standing in my bedroom doorway, poised to leave. "And you need to quit beating yourself up, Ridge. Musicians have blocks, just like writers do. You'll find your muse again. I love you."

"I love you, too."

She smiles and backs out of my bedroom. I groan, knowing she's trying to be positive with the whole writer's block thing, but I can't stop stressing about it. I don't know if it's because Brennan has so much riding on these songs now or if it's because I'm completely tapped out, but the words just aren't coming. Without lyrics I'm confident in, it's hard to feel good about the actual musical aspect of writing.

My phone vibrates. It's a text from Brennan, which only makes me feel worse about the fact that I'm stuck.

Brennan: It's been weeks. Please tell me you have something.

Me: Working on it. How's the tour?

Brennan: Good, but remind me not to allow Warren to schedule this many gigs on the next leg.

Me: Gigs are what gets your name out there.

Brennan: OUR name. I'm not telling you again to stop acting like you aren't half of this.

Me: I won't be half if I can't work through this damn block.

Brennan: Maybe you should get out more. Cause some unnecessary drama in your life. Break up with Maggie for the sake of art. She'll understand. Heartache helps with lyrical inspiration. Don't you ever listen to country?

Me: Good idea. I'll tell Maggie you suggested that.

Brennan: Nothing I say or do could ever make Maggie hate me. Give her a kiss for me, and get to writing. Our careers are resting squarely on your shoulders.

Me: Asshole.

Brennan: Ah! Is that anger I detect in your text? Use it. Go write an angry song about how much you hate your little brother, then send it to me. ;)

Me: Yeah. I'll give it to you after you finally get your shit out of your old bedroom. Bridgette's sister might move in next month.

Brennan: Have you ever met Brandi?

Me: No. Do I want to?

Brennan: Only if you want to live with two Bridgettes.

Me: Oh, shit.

Brennan: Exactly. TTYL.

I close out the text to Brennan and open up a text to Warren.

Me: We're good to go on the roommate search. Brennan says hell no to Brandi. I'll let you break the news to Bridgette, since you two get along so well.

Warren: Well, motherfucker.

I laugh and hop off the bed, then head to the patio with my guitar. It's almost eight, and I know she'll be on her balcony. I don't know how weird my actions are about to seem to her, but all I can do is try. I've got nothing to lose.

About the Author

COLLEEN HOOVER is the #1 *New York Times* bestselling author of *Slammed*, *Point of Retreat*, *This Girl*, *Hopeless*, *Losing Hope*, *Finding Cinderella*, *Maybe Someday*, and *Ugly Love*. She lives in Texas with her husband and their three boys. Please visit ColleenHoover.com.